HARD WAY

ALSO BY J. B. TURNER

J. B. TURNER
HARD WAY

THOMAS & MERCER

Published by Thomas & Mercer, Seattle

www.apub.com

Amazon, the Amazon logo, and Thomas & Mercer are trademarks of Amazon.com, Inc., or its affiliates.

ISBN-13: 9781477848722
ISBN-10: 147784872X

Cover design by Stuart Bache

Printed in the United States of America

For Andrew, Robert and Sarah,
with love

Prologue

It began at nightfall.

The cars were down to a crawl as they approached the police checkpoint. Dozens of officers had blocked off two lanes of Rockville Pike in Bethesda, Maryland. A long line of drivers—some still wearing government employee ID lanyards around their necks—waited patiently to be spoken to. Each and every one was waved through almost immediately. But one vehicle—a sleek BMW SUV—was directed to pull onto the shoulder.

The woman driving the BMW wound down her window. "What's the problem, officer?"

"How much have you had to drink tonight, ma'am?" an imposing officer asked.

The woman seemed surprised. "Nothing at all. I'm just returning from working late."

"Do you mind stepping out of the vehicle?"

"Actually, I do mind, officer. I've got a family waiting for me. And I'm late."

"Ma'am, please step out of the vehicle."

The woman shook her head. "Really?"

"Ma'am, I won't ask a third time."

The woman switched off her engine and stepped out of her vehicle. She was led away from the line of cars to the sidewalk. The cop held up a finger and slowly began to move it horizontally in front of her face. "Can you follow this, ma'am?"

The woman complied, her gaze following the movement of the officer's finger.

The cop asked her to walk in a straight line, heel to toe. She did so.

"I'm sober, I can assure you."

"Can I see your ID, ma'am?"

She groaned. "It's in my bag, in the car."

"If you could get that, ma'am."

The woman went to her car and brought back a black tote bag. She rifled through it and handed over her driver's license and FBI ID. "Are we good?"

The cop nodded as he stared at the license and then the ID. He cocked his head in the direction of a police cruiser. "Do you mind sitting in the back while I authenticate your ID, ma'am?"

"What do you mean authenticate? Officer, this is ridiculous. It's been a long day. And I'm asking very nicely to please let me get on my way."

"Ma'am, I'm going to have to ask you to do what you're told, or face being arrested. Do you understand?"

"Unbelievable. This has never happened to me. I only live five minutes from here. My kids will be staying up to see me."

The cop opened the rear door of the cruiser. "Get in the back of the car. We have reason to believe you've been drinking. And we also need to authenticate your FBI credentials."

The woman stood, hands on hips. "And if I don't get in the back?"

The cop stood holding the open rear door. "Final chance, or you will be arrested, ma'am."

The woman shook her head. "Goddamn!" She reluctantly climbed in the back seat. He handed her a portable breathalyzer. "Can you breathe into that, ma'am, while I'm checking out this ID. I just need to rule out any alcohol use."

"This is insane."

"*Ma'am, we have reason to believe that you've been drinking. Can you please breathe into this device?*"

The woman shook her head. "Reason to believe? I passed the tests on the sidewalk."

"*Ma'am, if you would just blow into this.*"

"*Just to let you know, officer, I'll be taking this up with your superiors in the morning." She took the breathalyzer from the cop, then held the device to her mouth. As she blew, her eyelids began to look heavy.*

"*Ma'am, are you OK?*"

The woman's eyelids flickered for a few moments before they began to close.

She was out.

The officer took the breathalyzer from her mouth and strapped her in with the seatbelt. Then he got into the driver's seat and pulled away slowly from the line of vehicles, heading north on Rockville Pike.

He afforded himself a smile.

The odorless, tasteless vapors of the fentanyl capsule, which had been released as she blew in, had incapacitated her within seconds. It seemed hard to believe, but the highest-ranking woman in the FBI had just been kidnapped in suburban DC.

One

Jon Reznick was sitting in the Rock Harbor Pub with a two-hundred-and-fifty-pound slab of a man who was breathing hard. His drinking buddy was the former police chief of Rockland, Bill Eastland, a close friend of his late father. Reznick ordered two more bottles of cold beer for them. He noticed Eastland kept glancing at the hirsute barman. Then Eastland leaned in close to Reznick.

"What is it with beards these days, Jon?" he said. "Every fucker seems to have one."

"It's a hipster thing, I think."

"*Hipster?* What the fuck is a hipster?"

Reznick sighed. "God only knows."

Eastland shook his head. "Your dad would've hated hipsters. Absolutely fucking hated them."

"Probably."

"In our day, and I'm going way back, it was only students, communists, or beatniks that had fucking beards. Even my dentist has a fucking beard these days. What the fuck is that all about?"

"God knows."

Eastland's eyes began to fill with tears. "I miss your old man, Jon."

"Yeah . . ."

"Your father . . . he was a great man. I fucking loved him. Lost count of the number of times he hauled my ass out of trouble. You believe that? Hauling me out of trouble?"

Reznick nodded.

"Vietnam, Jon. Viet-fucking-Nam. Just two young kids from Rockland, scared out of our fucking wits, with rifles. And people shooting at us that we couldn't even see."

"I know."

Eastland wrapped a huge arm around Reznick. "I know you do. You know what it was like."

Reznick nodded.

"Marines, man. US fucking Marines. Fucking A."

Reznick drank some beer as the bartender gave him a sympathetic smile.

"Can't believe he's gone. Always thought it would be me."

"He'd given up. He was drinking insane amounts."

"That he was. That he fucking was. That's fair."

"Just the way he coped."

Eastland dabbed his eyes. "He was a tough man, Jon. Toughest man in Vietnam. I'm telling you, he wasn't afraid of no fuck. And I'm telling you, that's the goddamn truth."

"He was a handful."

"A handful? You kidding me? He was like a madman when he got going. Once, we were on some R & R in Bangkok, we got into a fight. You know how it is, right?"

Reznick nodded, knowing only too well.

"A mass brawl. Me and him fought a gang of sailors. He knocked four out cold. Wasn't afraid of nobody." Eastland closed his eyes. "I'm sorry . . . I didn't mean to go on like that."

Reznick finished the rest of his beer.

"I remember, the day you were born was the happiest I'd seen him. He was across at the Myrtle to celebrate with a couple guys from the sardine plant. Man, he was so proud that day. Yeah." He bowed his head. "So proud."

It took Reznick the best part of twenty minutes to support Eastland the few hundred yards to the ex-chief's colonial home, its American flag flying. Once his long-suffering wife Veronica had gotten him inside, Reznick headed to his own home along the near-deserted streets. He walked past the abandoned sardine-packing factory his father used to work in. Then onto the dirt road that led to his house.

The moon was full and illuminated the path. The same path his father had walked a thousand times. Back to the house his father had built with his own hands. The same earth the old man had trod. Reznick imagined him after a few drinks at the Myrtle, heading back to the house but unable to shut out the images that had been seared into his mind in Vietnam. The maimed comrades. The blood. The fear. And the ghosts that would never leave him.

Reznick loved the house. The salt-blasted wood with the ocean-blue paint his father had covered it with. They had stayed in a one-bedroom apartment in downtown Rockland while his father built the house. Every waking hour, when he wasn't working, his father was building. Laying the concrete foundations. Sourcing the wood. He'd even designed the layout.

Reznick had lived in the house ever since. He planned to die in the house. And he hoped that, one day, his daughter Lauren would return to Maine and live in it, maybe with a family in tow. His father would have loved that.

Up ahead, in the far distance, Reznick saw a spectral figure standing on his front porch. He kept on walking. Who the hell would turn up at his door at this ungodly hour? He didn't get visitors.

As he got closer, the shadow materialized into a man, just standing and staring at the front door.

He wondered if the man might be a threat. But he knew that if someone from his past decided they wanted him taken out, the assassin wouldn't be waiting on his porch.

Reznick got closer. He could now see that the man's face looked ghostly white. He looked scared. He wore an ill-fitting gray suit.

"Are you Jon Reznick?"

Reznick walked up the stairs and pulled his gun out of his waistband, pointing it at the stranger. "Who the hell are you?"

The man put his arms in the air. "Please, I don't mean any harm. Are you Jon Reznick?"

"You mind explaining who the hell you are? You're on my goddamn property."

"I need your help."

"My help? I don't even know you."

"Please . . . You know my former wife."

"Your former wife? What the hell are you talking about?"

"My name is James Meyerstein. I'm a professor at Georgetown University in Washington, DC."

The name crashed through his head. "Meyerstein?"

Reznick most certainly did know Martha Meyerstein.

"Yes, my ex-wife."

Reznick couldn't picture this man being married to Martha. "Are we talking about the same person?"

"I'm talking about FBI Assistant Director Martha Meyerstein. I think something's happened to her."

Reznick put the gun away as he showed James Meyerstein inside. He knew Assistant Director Martha Meyerstein—a workaholic, no-nonsense operator, a bit like himself. She had deployed him on several FBI investigations over the years.

"This is a bit irregular," Reznick said.

"I'm sorry for turning up like this unannounced. My rental car broke down a couple miles from here. The tow truck company said I'd have to wait till morning."

Reznick motioned Meyerstein into the kitchen. He poured out two tumblers of Scotch and handed one to the professor. "You look like you need one."

Meyerstein knocked back the amber liquid and closed his eyes. "Thank you. Martha always spoke very highly of you. She never confided much about her job—especially since our breakup. But I know she was very grateful for your help on several investigations."

Reznick sighed. "Our paths crossed inadvertently at the outset."

"She mentioned you were . . ."

"An assassin?"

Meyerstein flushed.

"It's OK. Relax. What else do you know about me?"

"Just that you're the best at what you do."

"What else?"

"I know how you first ran into Martha and the FBI. She said you'd been set up by your . . . handler. Sent to kill a government scientist. But you didn't. You protected him. Then you handed him over to the FBI."

"It was a mess. But anyway, shit happens, right?"

Meyerstein nodded. "I've got to level with you. I'm scared. Scared of what's happened to Martha. And, to be honest, I'm a bit scared being here."

"I don't bite, trust me. Look, I really don't know how I can help."

"Martha once mentioned that in the case of the scientist, as a reprisal, the terrorists kidnapped your daughter."

Reznick stared at him, long and hard. The memories flashed back. His daughter trussed up on a boat off Key West, held by some Haitian crazies. He'd been lucky to find her alive, and it was thanks to Martha. Reznick had handed over the scientist to the FBI in exchange for the chance to find his daughter.

"I thought that, in light of that, you might know how to find Martha if that was what's happened to her."

Reznick said nothing.

"Look, I don't know if she's been kidnapped. I just know she's missing. I'm sorry, I'm not making much sense."

Reznick stared into his glass of whisky. "What exactly do you know?"

"What do I know? I don't know where to start. My head's racing with everything that's happened today."

"How did you find me?"

Meyerstein blew out his cheeks. "Earlier today I got a call from Martha's mother. Out of the blue. We haven't talked in a while."

Reznick sipped his drink.

"Anyway, that's in the past. She said she was worried—that Martha hadn't returned home last night."

"Is that unusual?"

"For Martha? Absolutely. It's quite out of character. The children were worried too. And she couldn't be reached on her cell phone."

Reznick wished the professor would get to the point.

"So, I tried but, not surprisingly, still no answer. I called a few mutual friends, but no one had heard anything from her."

"What did you do?"

"I called the FBI."

"Understandable."

"And I was put through to Roy Stamper. He's a good guy, works as part of Martha's team."

"I know Roy."

"Well, he said it was probably nothing. He said she was under pressure and was maybe taking a few days away from it all."

Reznick shrugged. "Sounds plausible."

"I know Martha. She doesn't just not turn up or take a few days off without people knowing." James Meyerstein jabbed his thumb into his chest. "I know her. This is out of character. It doesn't ring true."

The whisky was beginning to warm Reznick's stomach. "Maybe," he said.

"There's something else."

"What?"

"I could tell from Roy Stamper's tone that something was wrong."

"How d'you mean?"

"He wasn't very forthcoming."

"I think that's maybe just the way the FBI are. They won't want to unduly alarm you."

"I guess."

"So you how did you get my name and address?"

Meyerstein looked down. "My former mother-in-law retrieved it from the house phone. I asked her to look for your number. Your initials and address here in Maine were also scribbled on a calendar."

"I see."

Meyerstein shook his head. "Look, I think something has happened to Martha. And the Feds don't want to say."

"Listen to me, you don't know that. People don't turn up all the time. They disappear for a day or two. It happens. All the time, let me tell you."

"You're not listening. Martha isn't the sort of person to disappear without letting people know. She's incredibly responsible and reliable. Goddamn, I've called the hospitals all around DC. But nothing. This is so out of character."

Reznick let out a long sigh. "How can I help? She might simply be a missing person. A person that chooses to go missing. To disappear. Have you thought of that? Is it possible she's just snapped under pressure and headed off somewhere?"

"Never in a million years."

"*Never?*"

"I'm sorry about turning up like this. I feel such a fool now. I dunno . . . I thought you might help. The children are worried sick."

Reznick put his half-empty glass on the table and looked at his watch.

"Five past eleven. It's late."

Meyerstein sighed. "I need to get back to DC."

"You might have to wait. The next flight out of here isn't until six in the morning."

"Damn."

Meyerstein's cell phone rang. He looked at the caller ID. "It's Martha's mother." He pressed the green icon and answered. "Hi, have you heard anything?" He frowned and nodded. "I see . . . In the last hour . . . Look, I'm working on it. Call you back." He ended the call.

"Any word?"

Meyerstein took a few moments to reply. "There's been a development."

"What?"

"The FBI turned up a few minutes ago and confiscated her laptop and iPad. And they're moving my children to a safe house."

"Did they explain why they've confiscated her electronic equipment?"

"Martha's mother didn't say. But I need to go and get back to my kids as soon as possible." His hand shook as he slipped the phone back into his pocket. "The FBI think something is wrong, don't they?"

Reznick nodded. Time was of the essence now. "Possibly. Look, do you trust me?"

Meyerstein looked at him carefully. "Martha thought you were a man she could trust. She places a high value on trust. And loyalty. So yes, I trust you."

"I can't make any promises," Reznick said. "None at all. That's important to stress."

"I understand that. I just want your help. I want you to find Martha. I want you to help me find her. If not for me, then for our children."

"Then you've got to do exactly as I say."

Two

It was just past 1:00 a.m. when Reznick called in a favor from a former Marine turned aerial-photography expert, Don Bleeker, who agreed to fly them in his Cessna down to DC. It was a bumpy three-hour flight to Reagan. When they landed, Reznick wrapped his arm around Bleeker's shoulder. "I owe you one, man."

"Forget it," Bleeker said. "Take care."

Reznick and Professor Meyerstein walked through the terminal, then hailed a cab outside. "This is for you," Reznick said.

"I don't understand . . . aren't you coming with me?"

"No. I want you to call Martha's mother and make sure your family are safe and sound. That's all that matters right now."

The professor nodded. "Do you think they're still at risk?"

"As long as everyone is out of the house, they'll be fine."

Meyerstein rubbed his face. "This is crazy."

"Listen to me. Make sure your kids are safe. Then think about moving out of your own home for a while. We don't know what the hell is going on."

Meyerstein looked like he was struggling to take it all in.

"You OK?"

"I'm OK, Jon. Just find her."

Reznick watched James Meyerstein get into the cab, which sped away. He headed across to the Avis booth, picked up a rental car, and drove it away from the airport and into the suburbs. It was just before five o'clock when he pulled up outside a small home with a neat garden, well illuminated. He slunk down low in the seat and waited.

Just before six, a man emerged from the house holding a briefcase and speaking into a cell phone. Reznick watched for a few moments. Then he got out of the car and walked toward the man.

"Hey, Roy . . ."

Special Agent Roy Stamper spun around, phone still pressed to his ear. "I'll call you back." He ended the call and took a step toward Reznick. "What the heck is this?"

"I'd like to talk to you," Reznick said.

"You're outside my goddamn house."

"You made it easy, Roy. You need to switch off location services on your iPhone."

"Are you out of your mind? I could have the cops around here in a flash and you'd be thrown in jail, no questions asked."

"Roy, is that any way to treat an old friend?"

"You're not my friend, Jon. I like you. And I know we've worked together. But this is just way out of left field. What the hell were you thinking?"

Reznick sighed. "I was thinking why did you tell Meyerstein's ex-husband there was nothing to worry about? Now I'm hearing that your guys have taken all her computer equipment."

Stamper's eyes were blazing and he pointed at Reznick. "Let me make one thing clear. This has nothing to do with you, you hear me?"

"Doesn't it?"

Stamper pursed his lips and looked around the quiet residential neighborhood. "Last I looked, Jon," he said, lowering his voice, "you don't work for the FBI."

"You're not being totally honest with Professor Meyerstein, are you?"

Stamper flushed.

"You see, Roy, you might be a really fine special agent, but you're a damned poor liar."

"I don't have to take this. You're out of line. And I've got work to do."

Reznick stepped forward and stood in front of Stamper. He smelled the man's fresh cologne. "I don't play games. You should know that by now. I want to help you."

"Jon . . . this does not concern you."

Reznick didn't back down.

Stamper stared at him, then rolled his eyes. "Jon, I'm under a helluva lot of pressure. I need to get into work."

Reznick nodded once. "This can go one of two ways, Roy. The first way is the Feds deal me in. The second way is you keep me out. But if you go down the second route, I must warn you, I will investigate whatever has happened to her myself."

At this, Stamper seemed to regain his sense of authority. "Who are you to lay down the law, Jon?"

Reznick shrugged. "Your choice. You either have me inside the tent, or have me outside pissing in. Your call."

Stamper went quiet, watching him. Then he raised his cell phone and dialed a number.

"Sir, good morning, very sorry for disturbing you so early. I have Jon Reznick standing outside my house." He nodded. "Yes, that Jon Reznick. Thank you, sir." He ended the call and looked at Reznick. "That was the Director of the FBI."

"And?"

"He wants us in his office within the hour."

Three

The seventh floor of the Hoover Building was the most secure. It was where FBI Director Bill O'Donoghue had his office. It was strictly off limits to everyone, apart from those with the highest level of clearance.

Reznick and Stamper were escorted down a corridor and through airport-style scanners. O'Donoghue's secretary then showed them to the Director's door and knocked. She waited for a reply.

"Yeah, show them in," came a man's voice from behind the door.

Reznick followed Stamper inside.

Bill O'Donoghue was seated, working on some papers. He didn't look up for nearly a minute as Stamper and Reznick stood there in awkward silence. Eventually, O'Donoghue lifted his gaze and motioned. "That'll be all, Roy."

"Sir?"

"You heard."

Stamper glared at Reznick as he made his exit, shutting the door quietly behind him.

"Pull up a seat, Jon."

Reznick did as he was told.

O'Donoghue leaned back in his seat and fixed his cold gaze on Reznick. "What in God's name are you playing at, Reznick? You turned up at Roy Stamper's home? I've a good mind to have you arrested."

"Tell me about Martha Meyerstein."

O'Donoghue smiled expansively. "That has nothing to do with you."

"It's had everything to do with me since her ex-husband turned up on my doorstep late last night. And now it transpires that the Feds have confiscated items from her house."

"Jon, let me be quite clear. This isn't your concern."

"What do you know?"

"You're not listening, Jon."

"Tell me about Martha's disappearance. I'm not leaving until you tell me."

O'Donoghue shifted in his seat. "Who mentioned anything about a disappearance?"

"I did. And the fact that you had your guys turn up at her house and take away all the electronic equipment lying around, that's a definite red flag in my book. And you've moved the kids to a safe house."

O'Donoghue picked up a pen from his desk and pointed it at Reznick. "This doesn't concern you, OK?"

"Not OK. She hasn't just gone off on vacation or forgotten to go home, has she?"

"As I said, this doesn't concern you."

Reznick sighed but held his tongue, allowing a silence to open up between them.

"I have a very important meeting in a little over an hour. And I'm already behind with my preparations."

"Don't shut me out. Don't treat me like I'm an idiot. I know how these things work."

"You've done valuable work for us in the past, Jon, I know that."

Reznick nodded. He knew the Feds felt uncomfortable with any input from him. He was a trained assassin, after all. His methods didn't align with the legal structures and strictures the FBI adhered to. But Meyerstein had seen firsthand how useful he could be. "You've got a situation, haven't you?"

"I'm not at liberty to discuss operational matters with you."

"Listen to me. I'm on your side. I sometimes tell you things you don't want to hear. But if there's any way I can help you guys, and I mean *any* way, I'm saying deal me in. Don't shut me out. I appreciate that my position has never been appreciated by those over in Homeland Security. And certain sections of the FBI. I get all that. But that's no concern to me. I'm not even asking for official accreditation."

O'Donoghue sighed. "What do you want?"

"Just get me on the team."

O'Donoghue said nothing.

"She's been missing for nearly thirty-six hours and you don't know where she is, am I correct?"

O'Donoghue pinched the bridge of his nose and shook his head.

"This is your call, sir. You either deal me in or I'll be out there doing this by myself, my way. With people of my choosing. Your choice."

"This is the FBI, Jon. We don't do ultimatums. Your methods go against everything we stand for. You kill people. Do you understand what I'm saying?"

Reznick took a few moments to compose himself. "I'm here to help. I'm offering my services."

"Look, if you think you owe her or us because of your work with her . . ."

"I do owe her. A debt of gratitude."

"Jon, you don't owe her or us anything."

"That's where you're wrong. Her decision to flout your goddamn protocols gave me the chance to recover my daughter from that boat those fuckers were holding her on. You remember that? Down in Key West? I owe her."

"You need to let this go. We're dealing with a complex situation . . ."

"Which means what exactly?"

O'Donoghue got up and stared out of the window.

"Cut me in, sir. You know, sometimes having an extra viewpoint can be beneficial. I think I can help you get her back."

"We know what you can do, Jon."

"Three separate occasions I've helped you guys . . . What's the downside of getting me involved?"

"Legality . . . God knows where it could end up. Besides, if it leaked that you were on board . . . I mean, Jesus, you can almost see the headlines. Those bastards on Capitol Hill would have a field day with us."

"To hell with them. Let's focus on using everything at our disposal to get her back. What do you say?"

O'Donoghue sighed. "I know Martha has reached out to you in the past. But the problem is, you don't do boundaries. You don't follow the rules of the law. And that, for the FBI, is—putting it mildly—problematic."

"I don't mind problems. I can work around problems."

"You're not going to let this go, are you?"

"Not on this occasion. I'm not walking away. That's not what I do. But I can help you."

"We *will* find her."

"And what if you don't? Her intelligence knowledge could be invaluable in the wrong hands."

"You don't have to tell me that."

"No one need know I'm here, sir. Besides, we both want the same thing. Martha Meyerstein back with her family."

O'Donoghue stared at Reznick. "You're only here because I allowed it to happen. I decide what can and cannot happen. Are we clear on that point?"

"Very much, sir."

"This is how it's going to work. You play by my rules, OK?"

Reznick nodded.

"No fuck-ups. You can work alongside Stamper's guys. But only on the proviso that you don't hide anything from him. That's very important. He'll keep me abreast of everything and anything, do you understand?"

Reznick nodded again.

"I don't want leaks. Do you hear me?"

"Got it. What's happened to her?"

"Talk to Stamper. He leads. And, Jon, one final thing . . ."

"What's that?"

O'Donoghue fixed him with a hard gaze. "Don't fuck with me."

Four

Half an hour later, after being issued a temporary FBI badge, Reznick was escorted by the Director's secretary down to an operation room on the fifth floor. Stamper took him into a side room. There was a desk with a MacBook Pro, video footage of a police roadblock playing on the screen. A TV remote control sat beside it. Two chairs flanked the desk and a bank of huge screens covered one of the walls.

Stamper shut the door and sat down on the edge of the desk.

Reznick raised his hands. "I'm not here to make trouble. I just want to help any way I can in locating Martha."

"Did we ask for your help, Jon?"

"I'm offering my help. And the Director has accepted. Got a problem with that?"

"We do things our way."

"I'm fine with that, Roy."

"Make sure you are."

"So, what are we dealing with, Roy?"

Stamper sighed. "There's a media blackout on this. That won't surprise you."

"Understandable."

"Strictly need-to-know, even within the FBI. Everything goes through me. Clear?"

"Crystal."

Stamper picked up the remote control and switched on one of the screens on the wall. Staring down at them was a photo of a tough-looking, bull-necked man, tattoos scaling his neck.

"Who's this?"

"Joseph 'The Shark' Salerno. Capo for what remains of the Genovese crew in New York. Complete renegade. Psychopath. Degenerate. Killer. Armed robber."

"How does he fit into things?"

Stamper indicated for Reznick to watch the video on the MacBook. "We were given his name by two mafia sources."

"Where and when was this footage taken?"

"This was taken about thirty-six hours ago in Bethesda, out near where Martha lives. Fake DC Police roadblock."

Reznick watched as she was escorted out of her car and took several steps, heel-to-toe.

"Then she got into what looks like a cop car. But it wasn't. It was fake plates, sophisticated paint job. Very, very convincing."

"So she's been kidnapped by this guy dressed as a cop?"

"Yeah, absolutely. His brother was put away just over a year ago—extortion, murder, armed robbery, you name it. And he threatened to kill Meyerstein. The word was sent out. The crew Joseph Salerno runs with are not all mafia. But they are hardcore. From California, Texas, a couple of Aryan Brotherhood thugs . . ."

"Interesting."

"But the backbone of the crew he runs with is from New York. Queens, mostly. Staten Island, too."

Reznick watched as the footage ran again. "Very organized. They've done this before."

"This crew, their modus operandi is fake police roadblocks, usually to snare armored trucks they've targeted. This is what they do. And the fact that Martha put away their leader's brother after the armored-truck heist in Midtown Manhattan two years back—they got away with four million dollars—tells us what we're dealing with."

Kidnapping an FBI assistant director for payback? It wasn't as though that would give them the green light for future heists.

"The footage . . . Who took it?" Reznick asked.

"A driver who had a dashboard camera caught most of the action."

Reznick glanced up at the photo of the bull-necked mobster on the screen. "So this mafioso is one of the guys in this footage? And his brother is the one Martha locked up?"

Stamper pointed to the stocky fake cop, who was speaking into a cell phone in the paused video. "We've gone over the physical characteristics, and this guy matches Joseph Salerno's profile." Stamper sighed. "It's not good. Worst-case scenario, they've killed her already."

"How likely is that?"

"No one knows."

"Have you been in touch with the New York mob?"

"Absolutely."

"And what are they saying?"

"They're trying to find him as well. They think he's a rat. The word is out that they're gonna kill him if we don't find him first. We've hauled in ninety of their guys already, shut down a dozen scams they were working, you name it. And they're telling us they don't know anything about this, but this guy is as good as dead anyway for bringing the heat on them."

"So is this guy a fully iniated member of the Mafia?"

"He was. Technically still is. But there's a price on his head. Multiple sources saying they'll whack him on sight."

"But in the meantime an FBI assistant director is being held by these fucks? And we have no idea if she's dead or alive?"

"Right."

"And the Genovese family and their associates have not made contact with the FBI?"

"Why would they do that?"

"I don't know . . . perhaps to rub your noses in it. Perhaps to show who's boss. Perhaps, I don't know, they want to do a deal. A swap for their guy in jail."

"There's been no contact."

Reznick reflected on that. "Does that strike you as strange? More than twenty-four hours she's been missing, and nothing?"

"Jon, I've got to be frank with you, I'm fearing the worst. We all are."

Reznick began to pace the room. He looked up at the image on the screen. Then he stared again at the dashboard-cam footage on the computer. "Is that all we have?"

"We've got some cell phone footage taken from a dog walker late last night. Just shows what we have already, except a different angle."

"I want to have a look at it."

"Be my guest."

Five

Reznick was shown into a conference room where a young Fed was poring over the footage on a laptop, scribbling comments in a notepad.

"What've we got here?" Reznick said.

The guy stood up and shook Reznick's hand. "Special Agent Matthew Cornell, sir." He sat down again as Reznick looked over his shoulder. "This footage was taken by Mary Beth Milligan. She was walking her dog when she saw the stop. We were doing door-to-door yesterday and she showed us this footage."

Reznick said, "Run it from the start."

Cornell played the video again. It was shaky, as if the woman had been holding her cell phone with one hand. It showed clean-shaven toughs wearing police uniforms, a few directing traffic, a few more stopping and directing other motorists to the funnel at the side of the road, where it was barricaded off. "These guys appeared to know what they were looking for." They watched Meyerstein voluntarily leaving her vehicle. "The angle of this footage and quality, bearing in mind how far away this was taken from the action . . ."

"How far?"

"Nearly one hundred yards, give or take. It doesn't yield anything we haven't already seen."

The video lasted forty-two seconds exactly.

"These mafia guys have been doing this, on and off, for the best part of twenty years," Cornell said. "They're pros."

Reznick pulled up a chair beside the young Fed. "Play it again." He scanned the footage and watched as four men—three close to the camera, and one at the top right of the screen—directed traffic. He watched it over and over, seven times, absorbing, watching the signals, trying to figure out who was giving the orders.

Cornell sighed. "Not much to work with, I know."

Reznick nodded. "Yeah, no kidding. Play it again, but this time, slow it right down. I mean I want to see every frame, each split second."

"Forensics has already looked over this."

"And?"

"Nothing."

"Slow it down . . . the slowest you can make it. Can you do that?"

Cornell nodded and tapped some keys. Then the footage began to play in ultra-slow motion. He sat back in his seat and folded his arms, presumably having watched it once too often.

Reznick leaned in close. He was transfixed, trying to get into the heads of the crew involved. He could see they looked in good physical condition. They didn't look like the average DC cop. A different shape. They exuded a cold detachment as they directed the drivers and cars for the fake inspections. Then Reznick's gaze was drawn to the figure dressed as a cop at the top right of the screen, arm outstretched, showing which lane the waiting cars should join. "Freeze it."

Cornell did as he was told. "What?"

Reznick pointed to the man's arm. "Uniform is two inches, maybe three inches, too short on his arm."

Cornell stared at the grainy footage of the man's right wrist.

Reznick felt his heart rate hike up a notch. The bare white skin revealed the faintest trace of what looked like a blemish on the man's arm. "Zoom in on the area around that guy's lower arm."

Cornell nodded.

The move only showed heavily pixelated dark dots.

"Can you clean this up?"

Cornell tapped a few keys again, and zoomed in further on the highlighted area. Through the magic of advanced software, the grainy pixels revealed a distinct image on the man's arm. "It looks like a bird."

Reznick leaned in closer.

"It's got two heads," Cornell said. "It's like an eagle. What does this signify?"

Reznick felt a tightening in his gut. He knew exactly what it signified.

Six

Reznick cocked his head. "Pick up the laptop."

"What?"

"You're coming with me."

Cornell did as he was told and followed Reznick out of the room and down the corridor.

"Where's Special Agent Stamper?"

Cornell pointed to a corner office. "He's giving a briefing."

Reznick pushed open the door. He saw eight people around a large table, videoconferencing on the big screen.

"What the hell is the meaning of this?" Stamper snapped.

Reznick felt all their gazes boring into him. "Turn it off. I've got something we need to talk about."

Stamper looked at the faces on the screen. "Gentlemen, we'll talk later." He pressed a button on the desk and the screen went blank. Then he turned to Reznick. "You mind explaining?"

"There's something I want to show you."

Reznick was handed the laptop by Cornell. He placed it on the table and turned to the young agent, whose face was flushed. "How do I get this image up on the big screen?"

Cornell looked at Stamper, who dropped a pen onto the table as if annoyed at the interruption before nodding his approval.

Cornell brought up the cell phone footage they'd watched in the other room.

Stamper said, "So what in God's name are we supposed to be looking at? We know who we're dealing with."

"That's where you're wrong. You have no idea who you're dealing with."

Stamper's gaze lingered on Reznick. "Excuse me?"

"Just watch."

Everyone in the room watched the footage again. Once it ended, Stamper said, "And?"

Reznick signaled for Cornell to show them the enhanced close-up of the double-headed eagle tattoo. "Did you see this when you looked over the footage?"

A deathly silence filled the room.

"Do you know what this signifies, Roy?"

Stamper stared at the image and shrugged. "So we'll run it through our system. Hopefully be able to narrow down our list of suspects."

"I wouldn't waste your time. This guy won't be in the FBI's system."

"Why not?"

"This guy's a foreign national, I guarantee it. So you might want to try Interpol."

"How can you be so sure?"

"The double-headed eagle is a widely used symbol from a foreign power going way back. And I've seen it countless times on certain individuals. But this is not an Italian mafia tattoo."

"OK, so if it's not a Cosa Nostra tattoo—what the hell is it?"

"You're not dealing with the Sicilian mafia. You're dealing with the Russian mob, here in America."

Seven

What followed in the conference room was a blizzard of recriminations, simmering anger, and finger-pointing as the Feds tried to come to terms with being so badly blindsided by what was now being blamed on false information from mafia informers keen on implicating the Genovese family. Eventually, they ripped up the Italian mafia armed-gang hypothesis and focused on the Russian mob.

A team of the FBI's Russian experts was quickly assembled.

Special Agent Leonid Sperantsky, whose parents had been born in Moscow but left after Gorbachev's emigration reforms, gave some background. "The tattoo is quite familiar to hundreds of what we term the Russian mob. Also known to work with and overlap with the Odessa mafia—Ukrainian émigrés—who are based in Brighton Beach. Sometimes interchangeable. They are regarded as the preeminent post-Soviet criminal gang in America."

"They have tentacles all over the country," Reznick said.

Sperantsky nodded. "They've established links with Armenian and Israeli crime figures in and around Brooklyn. But they've also expanded into LA, where those same ethnic connections with Armenians and Israelis are in place. Very secretive. Protection rackets, loan-sharking, assassinations, narcotics traffic, fuel-tax fraud. Extremely violent."

Reznick watched Sperantsky as the agent's gaze wandered across the others. "Give me your assessment of who within the Russian mob could have carried this out."

"The kidnapping would have had to be given the go-ahead from one man."

"The boss?"

Sperantsky nodded. "Vladimir Merkov." He picked up a remote control and clicked a button. Up on the screen appeared a grainy black-and-white photo of a frail-looking guy getting out of a limo. "This is Vladimir Merkov, head of the Russian mob in America. A mythical figure who, until recently, hadn't been photographed since he moved to the US after the fall of the Soviet Union. This was taken in London by the British Secret Service. Rumors suggest he is in failing health, perhaps close to death. He is believed to reside part of the year in Palm Beach, but we haven't been able to definitively link him to any financial holdings. He has effectively disappeared in the US. His son, Dimitri, was recently prosecuted for money laundering, mob killings, and corruption of public officials. Serving ninety years."

Stamper cleared his throat. "I think you need to know one thing about Merkov before we go on."

"And what's that?" Reznick said.

"It was Meyerstein who helmed the case that brought down his son Dimitri just over six months ago."

Eight

In the hours that followed, the Feds worked frantically to set up surveillance on major players in the Russian mob. Monitoring messages and calls. Trawling databases. Observing known mobsters 24/7. Agents were speaking to Dimitri Merkov's ex-wife and kids.

"The problem is," Reznick said, "we don't know for sure why the hell the Russians would do this. It doesn't make sense. Are they looking for leverage? Do you think they might be looking to do a swap, is that what it is?"

Stamper listened intently. "There's been no contact with the FBI from Merkov or anyone on his behalf."

"We got any photos of Dimitri taken at the time he was sent down?"

Stamper nodded. "Sure." He pressed a few keys on a computer and a series of photos appeared on the screen.

Reznick studied the thickset thirty-something man wearing an expensive suit. He had a bodybuilder's physique, a deep tan. "He needs to lay off the steroids."

"Gym fanatic. Spends hours every day in the penitentiary yard, lifting weights. Someone who disrespected him was left brain dead after Dimitri smashed a steel weight through his skull."

"Nice."

"Was in solitary for a couple months afterwards."

"Visitors?"

"Just one."

"And who's that?" Reznick asked.

Stamper tapped another key and a picture of a man in a suit wearing dark glasses appeared. "Adam Chapman, his lawyer."

"Is he under surveillance?"

"Sure."

"What do we know about this lawyer? I'm assuming Dimitri gets a call or message to him, and from there things happen, or don't as the case may be."

Stamper sighed. "Pretty much. The lawyer is based in New York. Most of his work is for shell companies formed by associates of the Russian mob."

"Are you going to stake out this guy?"

"Jon, you're not running this investigation."

"I never said I was. I thought we were both on the same team."

Stamper nodded. "To answer your question—yes, we are aware of his movements, Jon."

"That's good. But is he under physical surveillance?"

"Sadly not. We do, however, have him under electronic surveillance. Cell phone, iPad, home phone, you name it . . ."

"Why in God's name is he not under physical surveillance?"

"This is where it gets complicated."

"Complicated? What the hell are you talking about?"

"A previous bug within his offices was discovered."

"Shit."

"Indeed. Apparently this lawyer has a firm who routinely sweeps his office and house for bugs. They discovered our bugs in lighting fixtures, electrical outlets, switches, and smoke alarms."

"How did you find out he'd discovered the bugs?"

"You're going to love this. A letter to the attorney general from the dirtbag lawyer himself, no less. FBI settled out of court."

"Fuck."

"So you see our problem. In effect, that avenue is blocked off."

"That lawyer very well may be a cutout."

Stamper said nothing.

"He's the intermediary passing on messages or instructions, I guarantee it. He's the conduit. Are there plans for Dimitri to take over in the future? With Merkov senior in failing health, would that make sense? I don't know."

"Chapman wouldn't be so stupid as to communicate directly with Vladimir Merkov."

"That's right. But there will be others he communicates with who are only a few degrees from Merkov. So we need to get tight on him."

"Jon, we're as tight as we can be without the Department of Justice hauling our asses into court."

"But I'm not officially part of the FBI, am I? And I know this stuff."

Stamper took a few moments to think it over. "I'll head up to the penitentiary and speak to the governor. In the meantime, get yourself to New York. But remember, Jon, if this goes south and you get caught, you're on your own."

Nine

Brent Schofield, the special assistant to the New York City Police Commissioner, sat at a conference table surrounded by other security experts, listening to the latest terror-threat briefings. He scribbled some notes as he mulled over the domestic intelligence analysis. He nodded as he looked over the six other men and two women assembled. Everyone was cut from the same cloth, because he had handpicked each one of them. His ten years in the CIA, including time as a station chief in Islamabad and Riyadh, had given him a keen eye for who had what it took to be an effective intelligence operative.

The hours began to drag as they heard reports from the undercover officers, also known as "rakers," who were embedded in minority neighborhoods. Neighborhoods like Bay Ridge, which had seen an influx of Muslim immigrants since the 1990s. It had previously been an Irish neighborhood, but most streets were now dotted with mosques, halal restaurants and butcher shops, and Muslim education institutions.

Schofield listened as a raker described the monitoring of daily life in a Muslim bookstore, as well as cafés and nightclubs. He also heard from the "mosque crawlers"—police informants who monitored sermons by imams. He heard about Pakistani taxi drivers. There had been a recent initiative to stop cars for speeding and broken taillights, which gave cops the chance to search for outstanding warrants. An arrest could mean leverage for the police to turn cab drivers into informants.

A lot of the work was carried out by officers who fit the demographics. Pakistanis would target Pakistani-American neighborhoods. Palestinians would target Palestinian-American neighborhoods.

It was a constant struggle to stay abreast of any developments.

His cell phone vibrated on the table. He checked the message. It read: *Need to talk within the hour. Usual place.*

———

The office was located on the twenty-second floor of a tower block in Midtown Manhattan. He rode the elevator up, got off, then pressed his thumb against the biometric scanner on the keypad beside the lone door. It clicked open and he went inside. Schofield headed through another security door and into a large, open-plan office.

The man he still addressed as Mr. Charles—a former director of the CIA whose company "consulted" with the Agency—had his feet up on a desk, smoking a cigarette, watching Fox News. He turned and smiled. "Hey, Brent, pull up a seat."

Brent did as he was told. "I got here as quick as I could."

"You still keeping those Brooklyn Muslims in check?"

Brent smiled. "Someone has to."

"Good for you. How's the family?"

"They're good. Kids are healthy. Alison is back teaching."

Charles stared at him as if trying to decode his true feelings. "Good to hear. Brent, I want to bring you up to speed."

"I'm listening."

"A situation is developing which might impinge on one of our most valuable assets in New York."

"I know the guy you're talking about, sir."

Charles dragged hard on his cigarette, blowing the smoke out through his nose. "What I'm about to tell you doesn't leave this room."

"Fair enough."

"I'm hearing that an assistant director of the FBI has been kidnapped. And they're going to be focusing their efforts here in New York."

Schofield already knew this through a contact in the FBI.

"Here's my problem, Brent. My company offers strategic geopolitical consultancy for those at the highest level within the CIA."

"So I've heard."

"You won't have heard, however, that I'm in charge of a special project. That project is to protect that high-level asset I mentioned. To see the big picture. My concern is that—"

"You think the kidnapping of this assistant director might spill over into the CIA's sphere of influence?"

"Precisely. Smart boy. This asset has links. And we very much need to protect him so he isn't caught up in this. We need to be alive to the possibility, remote I grant you, that our asset might be compromised as the FBI puts out a dragnet, trying to get their colleague back."

"What do you want me to do?"

"I've been giving that very question some thought. I want you to reach out to the CIA's guy in the Hoover Building. I think his name is Curt."

Schofield nodded. He knew the operative very well. "We go way back."

"I know you do. He wears his redneck tendencies as a badge of honor, but he's pretty solid. So it might be worth checking in with Curt—try to get an inside track on the FBI team who are trying to find their assistant director. Do you know what I'm saying?"

"I believe I do. Leave it with me, sir. I know how to play this. Are the FBI close to retrieving their AD?"

Charles leaned forward. "The FBI has wasted twenty-four hours investigating the wrong people, thanks to our good friends at the Cosa Nostra. But now the Feds think they know who's behind it."

"And do they?"

"Not as well as they think. And it's our job to keep it like that."

Ten

It was mid-afternoon and Reznick was crouched alone in the back of a surveillance vehicle on a cobblestone street in Soho, a block from the office of Dimitri Merkov's lawyer, Adam Chapman. He was glad he didn't have to accompany Stamper on the visit to the penitentiary in upstate New York. He thought it would be a waste of time. Besides, from the moment he saw the picture of Chapman and found out he was the only person in physical contact with Dimitri Merkov, he'd been certain this had to be the guy passing on messages to the rest of the crew.

He hunkered down. Minutes turned into hours. The fucker must still be working.

Reznick had learned from Stamper's team that Chapman had visited Dimitri Merkov the previous day and returned to his home in Tribeca that night.

He stretched a few muscles to avoid getting stiff. Slowly, outside the van, shadows appeared as the November light faded. He watched a couple head into a bar. The woman looked not too dissimilar to his late wife. The same skin tone, the same look in her eyes, happy in the company of her partner. His mood began to darken. His wife, Elisabeth, had died in the World Trade Center attack, only about a mile from where he was now. She had been high up when the first plane hit. She'd been trapped. And then, when the towers collapsed, she'd been pulverized to dust. Reznick had visited the site many times since. He had watched a new skyline being born from the ashes but felt conflicted. He wished for the whole site to be left alone.

Reznick pushed those thoughts aside as he again contemplated the audacious abduction of FBI Assistant Director Martha Meyerstein. He wondered if the kidnappers had been following her from the Hoover Building. It began to dawn on him that he had never heard of such a senior FBI agent being taken in such circumstances on American soil. It would have required planning. Extensive planning. He imagined such an experienced official would regularly vary her route.

He began to wonder if there was more to it. Was it possible that the Russian mob would do such a crazy thing? They had to know the fallout.

But there was something else bugging him.

Her route. Her address.

How would they have known in advance that she was leaving? How would they have known she'd be taking that particular route? He knew the FBI would have instructed their staff in countersurveillance. Meyerstein would have been well versed in changing routes and times of travel to avoid predictable behavior. Then again, perhaps the kidnappers had pinpointed a particular part of her route that she had to use every day.

The questions were already mounting up.

Reznick tried to think of Meyerstein at that moment. He pictured her being held out of sight. In a basement, perhaps. He could only imagine the fear she was experiencing. He'd seen firsthand the impact her sudden disappearance had had on her ex-husband. He thought of her parents trying to explain to their grandchildren. The terrible, aching emptiness when what you loved was taken from you. He'd felt that when his own child was taken.

A cab driver pulled up and started haranguing a cyclist, snapping Reznick out of his reverie. He wondered if Chapman would ever leave his office.

He was starting to doubt the guy was even still inside when a figure emerged onto the sidewalk.

The lawyer was wearing a fedora and overcoat, collar up.

Reznick watched as Chapman headed down the street. He waited a few moments before he got out of the van. He spotted the lawyer farther down the street and saw him catch a cab. It was headed uptown.

He memorized the license plate. A few seconds later, another taxi appeared and Reznick jumped in. "Stay with the cab two cars in front."

"Sure thing. Uptown?"

"Yeah. Don't lose them."

The cab crawled through the streets. For a couple of minutes, they lost sight of the taxi with the lawyer in it. Then Reznick spotted the other vehicle again.

"So what's with you and this cab? You following your wife?"

"Friend of mine left his cell phone at my place," Reznick lied.

"I see."

Twenty minutes later, Adam Chapman's cab pulled in near Grand Central in Midtown and he got out.

"Here's fine." Reznick handed the driver a twenty-dollar bill before exiting the vehicle onto a bustling Madison Avenue. He jogged for nearly a block as he tried to keep track of the Fedora-wearing lawyer in the dark.

Reznick turned onto Vanderbilt Avenue, on the corner of 42nd Street. He saw an entrance for Grand Central Station.

Up ahead, the lawyer disappeared inside an imposing building with a blue awning.

Reznick approached and saw he was outside the Yale Club. He crossed over and headed to a coffee shop that gave him a line of sight to the entrance of the private club. He ordered an espresso and a blueberry muffin. A couple of hours later, the lawyer emerged and jumped into a taxi again.

Reznick passed on the details to a backup surveillance team the FBI had arranged. Then his call was transferred through to Stamper.

"Any luck with the governor?"

"Not much. Dimitri Merkov spoke through the glass with his lawyer yesterday."

"About what?"

"Drawing up a new will, apparently."

"Nothing else?"

"They were very careful."

"Yeah, but that wouldn't stop these fucks using code words, right?"

"I get that, but the governor and his team are alive to that kind of thing, and they seemed to think it was just a routine visit."

Reznick sighed.

"Listen to me, Jon, we're monitoring this guy electronically. Whatever he says will be picked up either through Chapman's cell phone or his email. But we have to play by the rules."

"That isn't going to help you find Martha. Do you know where he is right now?"

"I have people keeping track of him."

"Can you get me a list of every member of the Yale Club?"

A silence opened up. "You're not giving the orders around here, Jon."

"I never said I was. I'm just asking you a civil question."

"Why on earth do you want that? Do you think Merkov is a member of the Yale Club?"

Reznick bristled at Stamper's tone.

"That's where our lawyer friend went after leaving his office."

"He might have gone for a meal. Perhaps a drink. It happens, Jon."

"Maybe. Maybe not. I'd like a list."

"Anything else?" Stamper's voice was dripping with sarcasm.

"Yeah, cut the fucking attitude. And pull up any surveillance footage inside the club from the moment Chapman walked in."

Eleven

Around midnight, Reznick was in the FBI's office on Federal Plaza in Lower Manhattan, half a dozen blocks from Adam Chapman's home. Just as he was being handed a black coffee by a young Fed, Stamper walked in.

"Roy, what the hell are you doing here?"

"Jon, I owe you an apology."

"For what?"

"My attitude. I had no right to give you such a hard time. I know Martha thinks the world of you. It's just . . . this whole thing is getting under my skin. I hope you understand."

"Happens to the best of us. Forget it." Reznick thought Stamper looked ashen. Eyes bloodshot, clearly not sleeping.

Stamper signaled for him to move into a conference room, shutting the door quietly behind them.

"Thought you'd be returning to DC," Reznick said.

"Makes sense to be based here. The lawyer is here. And Merkov junior is upstate."

Reznick nodded. "Tell me, what's the latest?"

"We're doing absolutely everything and we have nothing. I swear, the team is working every angle on the Russian mob—and Merkov and his associates—but we're nowhere."

Reznick took a sip of his coffee. He pulled up a seat and slumped down. "They're tight. They wouldn't divulge anything willingly. Let's go over the prison visit one more time."

"Governor was a pain in the ass, wanting to know why the visit from the FBI . . ."

"Hope you told him it was none of his goddamn business."

"Not in so many words, but yes."

"What did he say?"

"Made it known that he expected better cooperation, and that he'd be taking this up with the Director personally."

"Whatever. Anyway, did you get the Yale list?"

Stamper nodded. "Was just emailed through to me. We've run them through face recognition. Hedge fund types, lawyers obviously, a scattering of politicians, but every one of them is clean."

"Lawyers? Clean? Gimme a break."

"Jon, this is not the time for jokes."

"Did you get the surveillance camera footage from within the Yale Club?"

"The tech guys have a fifty-seven-minute stretch of video showing Chapman inside."

"Can I have a look at it?"

"Absolutely. As soon as they've finished editing, be my guest."

Reznick nodded. "There's a possibility Chapman is taking not only coded messages from Dimitri Merkov, but communicating instructions."

Stamper looked pensive, the strain of the investigation etched into the lines of his face. "So far as leads go, the lawyer is the only one we have. Let's hope he gives us the breakthrough we need."

Twelve

It was after midnight when Brent Schofield got off the F train and walked along East Broadway to an all-night diner on the edge of Chinatown. Inside, a man sat alone reading a copy of the *New York Times*. Schofield ordered two lattes and a couple of chocolate muffins, and set them on the table where his old Agency colleague was sitting.

Curt looked over the top of the paper, then folded it and put it down. "Man, you gotta be kidding me."

Schofield smiled and took a sip of his coffee. "Oh yeah . . . in the flesh."

Curt shook his head. "How you doing?"

"I'm doing good."

"Is that right?" Curt leaned forward, elbows on the table. "How long you been in New York?"

"Couple years."

"How you finding it, man?"

"It's OK . . . once you find your way around."

Curt grimaced. "Gimme Nebraska any day." He lowered his voice. "Fucking wall-to-wall liberals here."

Schofield grinned. He knew Curt had been like this since the first day they met at the Farm, when they were being trained up by the CIA. "It's New York, not Nebraska. It's always changing. That's what gives it the vitality. That's what they say, right?"

Curt grimaced. "You sound like you've been hanging out with a bunch of commies. *Vitality?* Gimme a fucking break, man."

Schofield fought the urge to burst out laughing. "You haven't changed."

"Damn straight."

"Look . . . I appreciate you meeting me at short notice. You busy?"

"Big time. Got a meeting in half an hour, if you can believe that. Feds are going crazy. Everyone's working their nuts off on this. Nearly a hundred extra agents in the New York field office."

That was all the confirmation Schofield needed. He got down to business.

"I've had a request from Mr. Charles."

"Charles? I'd heard he retired."

"He's still hanging around. I met up with him earlier. Here in New York."

Curt sipped his coffee. "Here in New York? Interesting. What did he want to know?"

"He wants me to open up a back channel link with someone in or around the investigation you've been assigned to . . . but more importantly, he needs someone who understands the nature of our business."

"You want me to be that back channel, is that it?"

Schofield bit off a mouthful of muffin. "We need to be kept abreast of any developments."

"You mind me asking why?"

"Your investigation may spill over into . . . shining a light on an asset of ours. A very precious asset whose identity can't be compromised."

"All right. What else?"

Schofield dabbed his mouth with a napkin. "We need to know exactly how much the FBI knows. I believe there's someone called Jon Reznick involved with this team in some capacity."

Curt nodded. "That guy is interesting."

"Was he the one that took down the Quds operatives a couple years back? At least that's what I heard."

"You heard right. Reznick's ex-Delta buddy was suicided in a car accident by Quds. Reznick went after them all. And he was the one that got the Feds involved."

Schofield nodded. The story was that Reznick had done off-the-books jobs for the Agency over the years. But now he was pretty much a freelance contractor.

"Killed the leader of the Iranian cell in a tunnel as he was headed to Mexico."

"So we've got to assume that Reznick is going to do the unexpected."

"He's dangerous," said Curt. "He's got them changing direction already and onto the Russian mob. His kind is relentless."

"That's a concern. From what I hear he's not known for doing dot-to-dot investigations."

"He'll do whatever he's hired to do. But this one seems personal. I don't think the bosses are entirely happy to have him there. We're both reporting to Stamper."

Schofield sipped his hot coffee, appreciating the rich taste and caffeine fix. "Is that right? Good to know." He paused as a waitress walked past. "Mr. Charles wants to be kept fully abreast of developments."

Curt nodded.

"But you've got to be very, very careful. This is important stuff. Don't ask questions. I want you to listen. Soak up what you hear. The direction of the investigation . . ."

Curt looked around as if concerned someone was listening in. He lowered his voice. "You know what we're investigating?"

"Yes, I do."

"This is heavy-duty shit. And they're pulling out every stop to find her."

Schofield leaned in close. "That investigation is small fry compared to protecting the national interest. There's something coming up and—" He broke off, enjoying the look of alarm on Curt's face.

"What exactly?"

"You know what we do. There's always one plot or another that needs to be stopped. We can't jeopardize our line of intel, or compromise the asset."

"I understand what you're saying."

"I've got to level with you, Curt. My concern is that someone like Reznick is going to be operating—sooner, rather than later—outside the direct control of the FBI."

"He kinda is already. By all accounts he's a de facto lone wolf on this."

"That's why we need to keep him on a tight leash."

Thirteen

It was the dead of night and Reznick was sitting alone in the conference room at the FBI's New York field office. He was still waiting for the tech guys to copy him in on the surveillance footage of Dimitri Merkov's lawyer in the Yale Club.

He ran things through in his head, thinking again of Meyerstein's route. Had they been following her for a while? The Feds had recovered tracking information from her car's on-board computer, which showed that she had driven a different route to the previous two evenings. She'd been doing the right thing. He began to wonder if her cell phone had been compromised—her movements monitored remotely.

Reznick stared at the picture of Meyerstein that was pinned to the wall. Her steely blue eyes reminded him of Elisabeth. But there was also the quiet determination in how she went about her business.

The FBI was second only to the NSA for electronic surveillance. But as technology and encryption improved, and as law enforcement agencies became more adept at digital surveillance of an individual or group, sometimes what got overlooked was physical surveillance. He knew from his CIA training at the Farm that the Russians were masters of tradecraft—the old-fashioned way of doing things. Communicating signals. Exchanging messages. Dead drops. Cutouts. And ex-KGB and Spetsnaz operatives were almost certainly well represented in Russian mob life.

Reznick gulped the dregs of a cold coffee as the phone on the table rang. He picked up. "Yeah?"

"Jon, footage ready to roll in Briefing Room A. Three analysts are checking it out. You wanna join us?"

"Appreciate that, thank you."

Reznick got up and headed through to the tiny office. There, he found himself looking over the shoulder of a senior analyst, Special Agent Ronnie Thomas, who was scouring the color footage.

They watched as Adam Chapman approached the Yale Club building. He swiped a card to get in, then the feed switched to an inside camera, which showed him heading into a locker room. He put on a white T-shirt, white shorts, and white Nike running shoes, placing his other clothes in a locker. When he emerged, he headed to Court Two for a game of squash with a middle-aged man with a paunch. Reznick watched Chapman's sinews stretch, his muscles defined.

The minutes went by. The more he watched, the more Reznick wondered if they were just wasting their time. But his instincts were always to persevere. And he knew from working with Meyerstein that she would be the same. She would never give up—she would dig in. What seemed like a lost cause might, just might, generate a lead. A sliver of information.

He'd lost count of the number of covert surveillance operations on supposed jihadis in Europe that he'd been tasked with monitoring that hadn't resulted in the intel they'd expected. But the longer a person was observed, the more of their character was revealed. Or links to other potential recruiters were established. And sometimes the surveillance even revealed a full cell structure, allowing all the members to be targeted.

On-screen, Chapman beat his opponent easily. They shook hands, patted each other on the back. Then the lawyer returned to the locker room, where he changed into some swim shorts. He swam twenty lengths of the Yale Club pool. When the footage recommenced, it showed the lawyer back in the locker room, combing his hair, examining a small shaving cut on his neck as he stared into the mirror.

Reznick yawned as Chapman walked back over to the lockers, but then stared at the footage as the lawyer opened a backpack and pulled out a book.

"What the fuck?"

He watched closely as Chapman placed the book in the end locker, farthest away from the door, then locked it, putting the key in his pocket.

"What the hell?" Thomas said, freezing the footage. "Motherfucker."

"This just got a helluva lot more interesting," Reznick said. He called Stamper over and Thomas replayed the footage of the book being left in the locker. "What do you reckon?"

Stamper watched intently. "That *is* interesting. But I'd like to see the footage once he's left the premises."

Thomas nodded. "Absolutely." He picked up a phone from the table and keyed in a number. "Becky, pull up any footage from 19:17 onwards. Got it?" He ended the call, turned to Stamper, and smiled. "I think we're on to something."

Stamper nodded.

Half an hour later, the rest of the footage was emailed through. It showed a figure entering the locker room wearing a hoodie. The angle made the person difficult to discern. Reznick looked at Stamper. "The way they walk, Roy, looks like a female, am I right?"

Stamper nodded. "Most certainly."

The woman went over to the locker where the book had been left. She opened it and then pulled out the book.

Thomas freeze-framed the image. "OK, that's something. That looks very much like a dead drop."

"I agree," Reznick said.

"You're convinced this is related to Merkov?" Stamper asked.

Thomas nodded. "Yes, I am, sir."

"What I can't understand is what's in it for Merkov to be kidnapping an FBI assistant director. This is not his usual playbook."

Reznick stared at the screen. "That's why we need to find out who this woman is and take it from there. I swear to God, Roy, Merkov senior is pulling the strings on this."

Fourteen

The morning sun streamed in through the windows as Vladimir Merkov was leafing through the obituary section of the *New York Times* in his twenty-second-floor suite in the Ritz-Carlton hotel, overlooking Central Park.

The names of New York movers and shakers. Businessmen. A famous chef at a Madison Avenue hotel. A Swiss fashion designer. A writer. He thought of the contributions they'd made to the city and country. He reflected on his own contribution to American life. He felt a sadness well up within him as he began to ponder his own mortality. He gave a hacking cough before he lit up another cigarette. It was strictly against doctor's orders.

Merkov knew it was too late to start worrying about his health. He had perhaps a year to live, maximum. The chain-smoking and hard drinking had taken their toll. His doctors, the best in America, had diagnosed terminal lung cancer. It was eating away at him. He felt it nip at him now and again. But the whisky and the morphine injections were keeping things in check.

He got up from his seat and stared out the window at the golden-brown foliage of Central Park in the fall. Red and yellow leaves drifting in the wind. Despite the billions laundered through hundreds of businesses across the world, tucked away in numerous Swiss and

Cayman Island accounts under fake names, he hadn't been able to buy immortality.

He dragged hard on the cigarette as gray-blue smoke filled the room. It seemed like yesterday that his beloved only son was walking with him in Central Park. He closed his eyes as he remembered the night they'd fled Russia.

He'd made his money during the fall of the Soviet Union, gobbling up oil and gas fields. It was like the Wild West back then. Everyone for themselves. But after a few years, he could see the way things were going.

The oligarchs were being rounded up. Or jailed. Or assassinated. He'd lost count of old friends who'd gone that way.

So he'd gotten out while he still could. He'd sprayed some money around at corrupt Russian officials. Had dozens of American passports made up. Then he'd simply caught a Gulfstream from a private airfield and flown to Germany. They'd refueled, and headed across the ocean to New York incognito. No one knew he'd arrived in America. He was under a false name. He disappeared.

He realized now how lucky he was. To have lived so long and to be dying a free man. But Dimitri, his wayward son, his only son—Dimitri's imprisonment weighed heavily on his heart.

Merkov turned and stared at the gold-framed photo on top of the TV. It showed his son on a football field at an exclusive New England prep school, throwing a bucket of ice over the coach as everyone laughed. It was hard not to look at the picture and smile. But it always pained him, too.

His son should have had a career, should have done better than his old man. But instead of knuckling down and getting good grades and heading to an Ivy League school, Dimitri had decided he wanted to join the family business. Money laundering, racketeering, offshore tax havens, violence, and murder. Merkov had tried to change his son's mind. But, oh, Dimitri was headstrong.

Merkov had regretted the decision ever since. He should have put his foot down and said no, that he wasn't joining his business or being introduced to his associates on the East Coast. He should have foreseen the outcome of his son's psychopathic tendencies. Dimitri seemed to like hurting people. Merkov always left that side of the business, by and large, to other people.

Merkov stubbed out his cigarette in a glass ashtray and stared out once more over the endless greenery of Central Park. This place was so far removed from his hellish upbringing in what was then Stalingrad. He remembered life among the ruins as a boy while the SS drew ever closer. They'd hidden. They'd lived off rats. They'd eaten human flesh to survive. And then they'd won the war. They had endured the unendurable.

Now look at how he lived. Five-star hotels. Homes in Aspen, New York, Miami, Los Angeles, London. He traveled on his own private jet. He was protected by a handpicked security team of former KGB officers, ex-Spetsnaz, and numerous ex-military bodyguards. He paid top dollar. And he expected—and got—the best.

No one fucked with him.

His only weak spot was his son. He'd given him everything. But because Dimitri wanted for nothing, he didn't give a damn. He didn't understand sacrifice. Discipline. Respect. Devotion.

His son knew only fast women, fast cars, and wanton, sadistic violence. Violence for violence's sake. Merkov wondered if his son, as a boy, had observed and absorbed the cold, detached persona of his father.

Merkov had realized he needed to rein Dimitri in. But by then it was too late. His son's torture chambers had been discovered in a Queens warehouse by the authorities.

It seemed unbelievable that a young man who could have taken over his father's empire without getting his hands dirty had allowed himself to be devoured by his demons. Let himself be destroyed. Incarcerated.

But that was in the past. The bonds of blood could be stretched but never broken. Merkov had plans for his son on the outside.

His cell phone rang and he fished it out of his shirt pocket.

"We have an update for you, sir." The voice was that of one of his closest associates.

"Go on."

"I think it might be prudent to move her."

"Already?"

"Better safe than sorry."

"How is she coping?"

"She's hanging in there. She's tough. So, when do we let the Feds know we have her?"

"All in good time."

Fifteen

The investigation seemed to Reznick to have been kicked up a notch. He was sitting at a conference table with half a dozen members of the FBI's New York task force. Stamper was standing with his back to a large screen. He seemed to have accepted Reznick's presence on his team.

He picked up a remote control and switched on the screen. An image appeared of a woman wearing a hoodie, which partially concealed her face.

Stamper cleared his throat as he looked at the stern faces around the table. "This image was taken at the Yale Club in Midtown. It shows a woman, approximately in her thirties. She opened a locker in the men's changing room and took out a book." He pressed a button on the remote control again and the screen split in two. "Here we have her on the left. And this guy on the right is Adam Chapman, who placed the book there."

Some of the agents scribbled down notes.

"We've been running this image through facial recognition software." Stamper pointed at a fresh-faced young agent at the far end of the table. "Agent Moodie, you want to elaborate?"

The kid flushed. "Yes sir. We've managed to find a perfect match. It took some time. But we got it via Interpol."

"Interpol?" Reznick said.

"Her face was in their files. She is in fact a British citizen. Her name is Catherine Jacobs. Apparently she began her career in real estate, became a millionaire, and eventually married Simon Jacobs, a London financier. Marriage collapsed and she moved to the States. Works for a bank. But get this. She moved, and remember she is a wealthy woman, to a rather small apartment in Brighton Beach . . ."

Stamper pinched the bridge of his nose. "OK, we need to get into this woman's life. We need to find out more about Catherine Jacobs."

Reznick said, "She's clearly either the cutout, or one of several cutouts they use to pass on messages and information. And I've got to say, this is very elaborate." A few nods around the table. "The problem is, while this might edge us closer to understanding how they communicate, it doesn't lead us at this stage to Meyerstein."

Stamper sighed. "This is going to take time, I'm afraid."

A female agent piped up. "The Russian mafia has connections to the Italian mafia, Irish mob, Jewish mob, and any other ethnic crime gang you can think of. It might be that another criminal organization is hiding Meyerstein."

Stamper tilted his head left, then right. "Possibly. But an operation this brazen could be compromised if another criminal entity, possibly with FBI informers within its midst, got wind of it. No, I think, on balance, this would be kept strictly in-house by the Russians." He turned and looked at Reznick. "What are your thoughts on where we are?"

"I'm concerned about the time that's elapsed. I'm concerned that the kidnappers haven't contacted anyone with demands. This is very worrying."

Stamper nodded. "Indeed. We're going to refocus our efforts on this woman. That's where we're going to catch a break."

Sixteen

Reznick popped a Dexedrine and washed it down with the dregs of his cold coffee. He was sat in the back of a surveillance van on 92nd Street, in the affluent Carnegie Hill neighborhood on the Upper East Side.

He zoomed in with the long-lens camera pointed at the entrance to an office building farther down the block. "Not a goddamn thing."

The surveillance operative monitoring the target's cell phone on a MacBook sighed. "She texted her mother seven minutes ago."

Reznick finished his coffee, feeling the residue of the Dexedrine dissolve in his throat.

"You got a sore head, Jon?"

"Not quite."

"You on medication?"

"Yeah, something like that."

The operative gave a wry smile.

"What?" Reznick said.

"Roy Stamper told me all about you. Said you're a bit of a character."

"Is that right?"

"Yeah . . . Said you brought down an Iranian crew in California a while back."

"You want to focus, son. There's an assistant director missing. Do you understand what that means? This is not the time for fucking around like some goofball."

"Yeah . . . I just thought . . ."

"How long have you been with the Feds?"

"Two and a half years since I graduated Penn State."

"Focus. And learn to observe. You got that?"

The rookie flushed crimson and nodded. "Got it."

Reznick was not a great fan of college boys and their good-natured ways. Pains in the ass. He'd much rather have someone on his team who had experience. He'd much rather have a hardened plain-clothes cop. Someone who knew when to speak and when to shut up.

He trained the binoculars on the sidewalk outside the bank as pedestrians strolled by. A few moments later, a thirty-something woman with a sallow complexion and wearing shades stepped out of the building. "Target on the move."

A second surveillance operative on the street said, "Yeah, copy that."

"Face recognition?" Reznick asked.

The rookie in the van said, "One hundred percent pass. You're up."

Reznick pressed his earpiece tight into his right ear. The surveillance van edged farther down the street and pulled up at a crosswalk. He jumped out of the van and caught sight of the target—Catherine Jacobs, a headscarf now wrapped around her head—heading west. When she reached Fifth Avenue, she did some window shopping before turning onto East 96th Street.

"GPS shows you're about ninety yards from her, Jon. Can you see her?"

"Yeah, copy that. Got a visual clear as day. Wrapped her hair up in some silk scarf thing."

"Very important that we not only know where she goes, but what she does when she gets there. So we need you inside the destination, unless she's just going for a stroll around the block."

Reznick pressed on through the bustle of the sidewalks, the blaring cab horns, and the hum of traffic. The smell of hotdogs from a vendor's cart made him realize he hadn't eaten in hours. He crossed the street as a cyclist braked hard.

"Hey, buddy, what the fuck!" the Lycra-clad cyclist shouted.

Reznick raised his hand to acknowledge him as he ran across the street. Up ahead, he spotted Catherine Jacobs heading into a building. He saw the engraving. "Oh cute," he said.

"What?"

"New York Public Library."

"What?"

"I'm telling you, these guys are good."

Reznick waited a while before he headed inside. He picked up a couple of books and pretended to look at the spines. Out of the corner of his eye, he observed Jacobs sitting at a table leafing through a coffee-table book. He noticed her bag was on the floor beside her. She sat for several minutes before she picked up the book and placed it back on a shelf. Then she headed down one of the stacks, partially hidden from sight.

Reznick moved closer and saw that Jacobs had bent down and gotten the book out of her bag. He saw the title in big black writing—*The Brothers Karamazov* by Dostoyevsky. Russian author. How very clever. She slid it onto the bottom shelf on the left. Then she got up and pretended to browse the shelves again. Reznick turned and faced the nearby shelves so his back was toward her.

The woman behind the circulation desk smiled at Jacobs. "Can I help you, miss?"

"Just browsing. See you later," Jacobs said, and she headed out of the library.

Reznick flicked through the pages of a random title, heart pounding. He waited until she'd disappeared from sight. Then he put the book back.

A minute later he emerged onto the street.

A crackle in his earpiece. "Jon, we see you. Anything?"

"Where's she going?"

"We're assuming back to the office."

"She just did a dead drop. Book. *Brothers Karamazov*, bottom shelf, left side of the classics section."

"Copy that."

"We need to get an operative inside and see what happens to the book. Until then, we draw back."

Seventeen

In the minutes that followed, a fresh two-man surveillance team took the lead and tracked Jacobs back to her office. A young female agent headed into the library. Reznick went into a sandwich bar with a line of sight to the library, and wolfed down a pastrami sandwich and a Coke.

Twenty minutes later, there was a voice in his earpiece. "Approaching from the east, big guy, carrying a plastic bag. You see him, Jon?"

He spotted the man across the street, heading into the library. "Copy that."

"We're running face recognition on this guy as we speak. Stand by."

Reznick wiped his mouth and hands with a napkin, feeling refreshed. He popped another Dexedrine. He was ready.

"Stand by . . . I repeat, stand by."

Reznick shifted in his seat.

A short while later, he heard a new voice in the earpiece. "We got something," whispered the female operative inside the library. "Male target has taken the book and put it in his bag. As cool as you like."

The minutes dragged and dragged as they waited for the man to emerge.

Reznick checked his watch. "Four minutes and no visual on the target." He got up from his seat. "We got the front entrance covered?"

"Three operatives in and around the vicinity," a Fed's voice said.

Reznick headed out onto the street. "How long since the book was switched and he left sight of the surveillance inside?"

"Four minutes and ten seconds."

"Fuck."

"Relax, Jon. Our agent inside saw him. Probably just stopped to take a piss."

Reznick hurried down Lexington and then turned onto East 95th Street. "Fuck."

"Jon, talk to me."

"How long?"

"More than five minutes. Nearly six."

"Fuck! The guy's given us the slip."

"Copy that, Jon."

Reznick began to run down the street, trying to get his bearings. "He's given us the slip. Motherfucker! Fire escape or some basement exit. Can't believe I didn't see this coming."

"Relax, we'll get him. Where are you?"

Reznick climbed on top of a parked car. He scanned the distance. Suddenly, at a crosswalk a hundred yards or more away, he saw the target's huge frame. "Got him. Crosswalk, Park Avenue."

"Do not fucking lose him, Jon."

Reznick sprinted down the sidewalks, barging past passers-by, some swearing at him, some getting out of the way. "Within one hundred yards. Target headed west along East 97th Street."

His earpiece crackled again. "All units, East 97th Street, Reznick on foot. Proceed with caution."

Reznick crossed over to the other side of the street as he slowed down to keep an eye on the target. He watched as the man headed up some steps and disappeared from sight. He crossed the street and saw the plaque. "Fifteen East 97th Street."

"Say that again?" Stamper said.

Reznick looked up at the church spires. "Fifteen East 97th Street. You know what it is?"

"What?"

"Russian Orthodox Cathedral."

Eighteen

Martha Meyerstein was traveling in darkness, trussed-up and blind-folded in the trunk of a car. It hit a pothole and it jolted her body. "Shit."

She had been trying to suppress the feelings of panic that were washing over her. She'd been hyperventilating earlier and had nearly passed out. But her training had kicked in and she'd begun to get on top of her fears.

The fear of the unknown. The fear of the dark she'd had since childhood. The fear of her fate. What were they going to do with her?

She felt herself begin to disassociate. She was drifting away. She wondered about her children. She knew Jacob wouldn't deal with it well. She pictured his eyes filling with tears. He was sensitive—he needed his mother close. Maybe because of how little she saw of him, mainly at weekends. But their time together, watching films, was precious. And what of Cindy? Her daughter was now more resilient. She saw the way Cindy had matured over the last year. She was a teenager. Fourteen. Slightly headstrong. Determined. Not unlike her own mother. She knew Cindy would reassure Jacob that everything was going to be fine. That was a crumb of comfort. What would they be thinking? How would they be coping?

She wondered how her mother was taking it. And her father. He'd take it the worst. She imagined him flying down from Chicago to DC to be with her mother and the grandkids. That was one thing. Her father would organize the family. Hopefully he would get everyone back to Chicago. Whoever had abducted her likely knew where she lived. But she found some comfort knowing that FBI protocol would have been for her family to be taken immediately to a safe house, far from harm.

She began to calm her rapid breaths. O'Donoghue would have had a task force up and running the minute they realized she was missing. She could only hope an FBI search team would find the information she had stored in her home. And that from there they could track her down.

She began to think of how she could escape. She struggled to try and get free. But she was tied tight. She wondered if she would get a chance when they opened the trunk. To lash out and grab a gun. She had to do something.

Her mind drifted. Every time she marshaled her available senses to try and piece together any clues—the tail end of an overheard whisper; a whiff of woodsy cologne; the expansive dimensions of the trunk—a different concern intruded on her thoughts. Was her hellish predicament proof of what she'd suspected but hadn't raised with the Director—that sensitive investigations were being compromised?

In the past months, Meyerstein had begun to be more circumspect with her team, unwilling to share her innermost thoughts about the investigations she was overseeing. She'd distributed even innocuous details on a need-to-know basis. It had begun with the collapse of the long-standing investigation into the criminal empire of Vladimir Merkov. Her team had received information about his whereabouts on three separate occasions. But when they'd turned up, there was no sign of Merkov or any of his crew. It was like he was always one step ahead, as if he were being fed information from directly within the FBI. The people who knew about the investigation were the in-house team, those at the most senior levels within the FBI, and a handful of people from other intelligence agencies who were assigned to the Hoover Building.

Meyerstein wondered if she was indeed in the hands of the Russian mob. She had put Vladimir Merkov's son away. Was this a direct reprisal? Leverage to get him released? Everything she knew about the Merkovs told her that this wasn't the sort of crazy move they'd make.

But that other concern nagged at her. Regardless of whether she'd been taken by Merkov or by someone else, someone in the FBI—someone she worked alongside, someone she trusted—had betrayed her. This struck right at the heart of what the FBI was all about. The integrity. The commitment. She needed to trust those around her. But recently, she hadn't been able to.

Her mind flashed back to being apprehended by what she'd thought were cops. She realized how unlikely it was that they had followed her movements. She changed her route regularly. She was a careful person. Did this point to a mole within her inner circle, tipping off the kidnappers?

The vibration from the car engine had ceased. The sound of metal, like chains. She felt a rocking and swaying sensation as if they were at sea. Creaking metal. Low voices like those of her captors. A jolt. Time dragged. She felt sick. Terrified. What was her fate? Were they going to dump her at sea? The sound of the car engine starting as the trunk began to vibrate. She rolled in the trunk as if going up a sharp incline. She sensed they were on the move. She began to drift away.

Suddenly the trunk popped open. Harsh lights. Bad aftershave. She felt herself being lifted. Heard grunts.

Eventually, she was carefully placed on a hard, wooden seat. She felt herself being tied to the chair. Ankles first, then wrists. She felt the ropes biting into her skin.

She sensed people were watching her. Harsh lights again.

"Welcome, Martha Meyerstein of the FBI."

With that single sentence, spoken with a hint of a Russian accent, her suspicions were confirmed.

"Go to hell," Meyerstein snarled.

"Rest assured," the voice continued, "you will be well looked after here."

Nineteen

The imposing man Reznick had followed finally emerged from the Russian Orthodox Cathedral and walked to Park Avenue. He stepped onto the curb and hailed a cab.

Reznick spoke into his lapel mic. "I got this." He read out the license plate number.

Stamper's voice responded in his earpiece. "We've got a match for this guy, Jon."

"Who is he? Is he connected?"

"He's a thug. A Russian mafia boss. Andrei Brenko."

Reznick felt his pulse racing. He hailed a passing cab and jumped in. "The taxi four vehicles ahead, don't lose it."

The driver glanced in the rearview mirror. "You a cop?"

"Just drive, my friend."

"Suit yourself, buddy. You're paying, right?"

Reznick kept his eyes fixed on the vehicle up ahead as they drove southbound to Midtown. There he watched Brenko jump out of the taxi. Reznick handed the driver a twenty-dollar bill and scooted out, then jogged through the crowds. They were close to Times Square.

"Jon," Stamper said, "you on foot?"

"Target's on West 44th Street." Reznick pushed through the throngs on the sidewalk. He caught a glimpse of Brenko entering one of the buildings. "Stand by." He got closer. "Yeah, he's just headed into a bar. Looks like an old-school place. Jimmy's Corner. You copy that?"

"Copy that. I'd like you to just hang back and we can observe."

"Roy, listen to me. With respect, I disagree. Time is running out. We need to push this thing. We need to know what he knows. Who's called this guy? And I know how we can get this information."

"No, Jon, you listen to me. This is how it's going to work. We'll put a surveillance guy in there and we can pick it up once he leaves. Far less intrusive."

"I've got a better idea."

"Jon . . . Don't do this, Jon. This is too important to compromise the operation. We need cool heads."

Reznick weighed up his options for nearly a minute. "Get a car out front, now."

"Jon, this is rash. I don't want you going in there, dragging him out, and this resulting in Martha's situation being compromised in any way, do you understand?"

"That's not what I had in mind."

Reznick took out the earpiece and shoved it into his jeans pocket. He popped another Dexedrine and headed into Jimmy's Corner. Inside was a long, thin bar. Boxing memorabilia on the walls. A few weathered drinkers in the booths. He walked up to the bar while his gaze scanned the drinkers. He spotted the Russian sitting alone in a booth, with a large beer and a shot.

The barman was chewing gum. "What can I get you?"

"Heineken. And a Scotch."

"You got it."

The barman poured the whisky and handed him a cold bottle of beer. "Where you from?"

Reznick felt the amphetamines rousing his system. Sharper. Harder. More alert. Switched on.

"I'm from outta town. I'm working nearby."

"Yeah? Where you from, man?"

"Up north."

"Got a brother who lives in Vermont. Fucking loves it. Fresh air and all that. You been there?"

Reznick nodded and gulped some of the beer. Then he knocked back the Scotch. He felt the amber liquid gently burn his insides as it mixed with the amphetamines. He felt himself grinding his teeth and took another drink of Heineken. He felt wired. He had the edge. He loved that feeling.

The minutes seemed to slow. The conversation from the men in the closest booth touched on politics, then veered to boxing talk. Reznick's father had preferred Roberto Durán over Ali and Frazier. He'd always followed the fortunes of the tough-as-nails little guy from Panama. He loved the way he didn't box his opponents, he battered them relentlessly. Slugging it out. It didn't matter if he was hit or cut or on the ropes. He'd slugged it out.

Reznick finished the Heineken and spotted the Russian in the mirror checking his phone. Was he sending a message to someone?

The goon got to his feet and headed to the back. He was going for a leak.

Reznick counted down from ten to zero and then followed the guy. He went down the long bar and saw the men's bathroom door swing shut. He pushed it open.

The Russian was standing, taking a piss. He turned and grinned. "OK, my friend?"

Reznick walked up to him and smashed his head against the concrete wall. The guy slumped to the floor. Reznick stomped hard on the man's jaw. It made a cracking sound, and the guy's eyes rolled up into his head. "I'm not your friend," he snarled, pulling him upright by the hair.

The Russian grimaced.

Reznick punched the man repeatedly in the mouth. Blood poured down the man's face. He dropped the man to the ground and stomped again on his face until the guy blacked out.

The Russian lay on the tiled floor, blood oozing from his head wound.

Reznick reached down and rifled through the man's pockets. He retrieved the cell phone and placed it in his own pocket. He washed and dried his bloodstained hands, checked his reflection in the mirror. Eyes cold.

He walked out of the bathroom and headed back through the bar toward the exit, nodding to the barman.

The barman smiled. "You off already, man?"

Reznick nodded again and walked out the door.

Twenty

Brent Schofield was waiting in an outer office of the New York City Police Commissioner, ahead of a security briefing, when his cell phone vibrated in his jacket pocket.

"You OK to talk?" It was Curt.

"Go right ahead. Where you calling from?"

"I'm calling from a deli, if you must know. A block from the office."

"Secure line?"

"CIA cell phone."

Schofield smiled. "What's on your mind?"

"You said you wanted to be kept abreast of any developments?"

"What's up?"

"Just hearing that Reznick and the surveillance team have got a result."

"What kind of result?"

"This is what I know . . . Reznick and a surveillance crew tailed Dimitri Merkov's lawyer to the Yale Club."

"Go on."

Curt explained the sequence of events.

"Hang on, and the Feds have put all this together?"

"You got it."

"Christ."

"Reznick is the driving force. He wanted them to get down to street level and take it from there, instead of electronic surveillance. He doesn't play by their rules. And it sure as hell isn't the usual Fed modus operandi."

The Police Commissioner's secretary popped her head around the door. "He'll see you now."

Schofield nodded. "Curt, gotta go. Keep in touch. And let me know what else transpires."

Twenty-One

When Reznick returned to the FBI's Lower Manhattan field office on the twenty-third floor of Federal Plaza, he was shown into a small room where Stamper was sitting behind a desk.

"Shut the door, Jon," Stamper said.

Reznick did as he was told and pulled up a seat. He sensed his actions at the bar hadn't been how Roy Stamper would have liked things to progress.

"Jon, you're going to give me a heart attack if you pull stunts like that."

"Roy, we got his phone. Forensics is analyzing the SIM card as we speak. So let's see where it leads us."

Stamper sighed and shook his head. "Our number-one priority is finding Martha. But I don't think your actions have brought us any closer to finding Martha, do you?"

"No, you listen to me, Roy. You're so fucking wrapped up in rules and regulations, you're fighting this battle with one hand tied behind your back. The NSA is great at listening in to cell phone conversations, tracking people, and all that shit. But I can guarantee, with guys like these, they'll be using new phones—once, maybe twice a week. Who knows, maybe every day, new phone. And then it's wrapped up in military-grade encryption. They might be using code phrases or words. Don't you understand that?"

"Of course I damned well understand that."

"We need to find Martha Meyerstein before she ends up in a body bag. Do you appreciate that?"

Stamper stood up and went over to the window, staring out over the city. "This is not how we do things."

"Listen, Roy, you made the right call when you said we don't want to compromise Martha's situation even further by dragging the Russian out of the bar. That would have alerted those higher up the chain in this organization, and they would've moved Martha. But this guy was using his cell phone in the bar. Maybe to message or email, I don't know. He'll just think he's been mugged in the bathroom of a New York bar. It happens, right?"

"It's illegal, what you did."

"No kidding."

There was a knock at the door.

"Yeah," Stamper shouted.

A young man came in. "Sir, sorry to bother you. The Russians have made contact."

Stamper turned around. "How?"

"They've sent us some footage."

Reznick's stomach churned. "Fuck."

"Channel thirty-two. I must warn you, sir, it's pretty graphic." The kid shut the door on his way out.

Stamper went over to the desk and picked up a remote control. He switched the TV on the wall to channel 32. His boss appeared on the screen. Face defiant. Gun to her head.

Reznick felt anger tighten every sinew in his body. "Motherfuckers!"

Reznick and Stamper watched as they played Russian roulette with her.

Then a voice with a Russian accent said, "You have forty-eight hours to release Dimitri Merkov. Otherwise, the next video you watch will show her brains getting splattered all over the walls."

Twenty-Two

The sight of Martha Meyerstein enduring Russian roulette at the hands of such thugs had enraged Reznick. He headed down a corridor. Then he was frisked by a security team, before being ushered into the corner office the Director had been allocated in New York.

Bill O'Donoghue was sitting behind a huge desk, dictating notes for a White House security briefing to a young male agent. "That'll be all for now, Agent Williams."

Williams nodded. "Yes sir." Then he turned and left the room, shutting the door quietly behind him.

Reznick took a step forward. "Are you aware of the new footage?"

"Who the hell do you think you're talking to?"

"Sir, with all due respect, I just want some answers."

"Then you learn to follow some basic rules when you're in my company. Is that understood?"

"Sir."

"Have I seen the footage? Yes. And I know from long experience in the intelligence community that this is not the time to overreact, Jon. We need cool thinking, rational thought."

Reznick pulled up a chair. "Sir, I couldn't agree more. Let's look at what we've got. We now have confirmation that they want to trade Dimitri Merkov for Meyerstein. They've made their terms crystal clear. And I say we should swallow some humble pie, and do what we have to do. So, we need to talk to them and open up a channel of communication."

"What's there to talk about? We don't do deals."

"Sir, I understand the logic of not wanting to do deals with people like this. I understand the FBI is all about upholding federal laws and investigating major crimes, but I've got to say, your position on this—bearing in mind we're talking about Meyerstein's life on the line—is, to me, pretty bewildering. I don't understand it."

O'Donoghue looked at his watch. "I have a videoconference with Homeland Security in five minutes."

"Why the hell are we not just making the deal?"

"The reason we're not making the deal is that they can't be trusted. And it's not what we do."

"And you think leaving Martha Meyerstein at the mercy of the Russian mob is acceptable?"

"That's enough! We don't do deals with murderers. We will find them. And we will find her."

"When? Sir, we're nearly out of time. They've given us forty-eight hours."

"I'm well aware of that."

"The rationale for doing nothing is just plain by-the-book bullshit and you know it. And it's the wrong call."

"So what do you suggest? Should we let Dimitri Merkov go free?"

"Why the hell not? Get him tagged. See if they'll settle for that. Do the deal. And deal with the fallout later."

O'Donoghue stared at him. "I've listened to what you've had to say, Jon. And I appreciate your candor. But we've got this. Be thankful you're part of Stamper's team. Is that everything?"

Reznick rose slowly and stared down at the Director. "This will not end well—trust me."

Twenty-Three

Reznick felt frustrated with the FBI's rules, regulations, and procedures. He was used to being given a job, usually an assassination, and carrying it out. Nice and simple. But working with the FBI was suffocating. They were hidebound by their ways of doing things. The FBI was beholden to the law, even if it meant their assistant director would die if they didn't find her.

Reznick felt stifled. He missed the control. His natural instinct was to go around the rules. In his world, the end justified the means. He would have much preferred to have made the deal with Merkov and gotten Martha back in one piece. In his world, doing the simple things was usually best. In this case, handing over a Russian mobster in return for Meyerstein was a no-brainer. Do it. And get her back to her family.

"Reznick, you wanna join us?" It was Stamper, who was holding open the door to a conference room. "It's important we focus. We think we've got a development on the Russian thug's cell phone."

Reznick headed into the room and sat down. Around the table, surveillance crews and FBI specialists were all staring at a huge video screen showing a guy wearing a polo shirt.

"Afternoon, New York," the guy said. "Special Agent Jimmy McDuffie."

Stamper nodded, then turned to face the room. "Special Agent McDuffie is our top guy down at Quantico when it comes to examining digital evidence. He's been examining data from the cell phone of the Russian mobster who was working as a cutout. Jimmy?"

"Since we got this cell phone and particularly the SIM, we've gone over it with a fine-tooth comb. Every contact is listed under a fake name. We checked the ingoing and outgoing calls and messages, and cross-referenced the numbers against the NSA's records. Every call has been from either in or around New York."

Stamper nodded. "What else?"

"We're looking for patterns. Nothing concrete, but we've detected Russian phrases. So we're talking Russian mob, no questions. Either known associates or prime movers. The frustrating thing is that they're clearly covering their tracks. Calls and messages were wrapped up in advanced encryption, which we've stripped away, but there's nothing really standing out. There was, however, something that got us interested. And we've checked this numerous times."

Stamper cleared his throat. "And what's that?"

"We checked the geographical identification metadata."

"Geotagging?" Stamper said.

"Correct. And we've been able to determine the locations visited by people who have either called this cell phone or received messages or calls from it. Common factors? The Ritz-Carlton, Central Park, New York City. We have eight separate instances geotagged right there."

"Jimmy, good work. Send us the exact times and dates those phones were logged at the Ritz-Carlton." He ended the video call and looked at Reznick. "It seems only right that since you obtained this cell phone, perhaps through nefarious means, you might want to comment."

Reznick blew out his cheeks at the barbed comment. "Let's hack into the Ritz's system and get the footage we need. Perhaps, at a stretch, speak to the head of security at the hotel and let him in on this. Need-to-know basis."

"That might be problematic."

"How come?"

"This is a very sensitive investigation. Very, very sensitive."

"We don't need to tell him the full story."

"He'll need to be convinced that the FBI should be prying into surveillance footage—unless we get a court order or something like that. And that takes time."

Reznick shook his head. "Need to be convinced? Jesus H. Christ, Roy, are you kidding me? Hack into the fucking system!"

"That's not how we do things, Jon. We work according to the law."

"Well, that's nice for Martha."

Stamper sighed. "I've cut you some slack. And you're still giving me grief."

"Roy, the time for rules, regulations, and worrying about all that bullshit is not here and now. Getting court orders is time-consuming, and so is getting the approval of the hotel. You need to make this happen." Reznick looked around the table. "I know you guys might not want to hear stuff like this, but from my side of the fence, you either get on this or be left behind. The only reason we've got this fucking bullshit lead is because I went in and got it. We didn't have any leads before, right?"

Stamper's eyes were hooded, not liking what he was hearing.

"Listen, guys, I'm not here to bust your balls. I'm not here to rile up Special Agent Stamper. But we all want the same thing. The return of Assistant Director Martha Meyerstein."

Nods from everyone.

"The kidnapping unit is working its guts out on this." Reznick pointed across to the agent in charge of the group. "How's that going?"

The agent blew out his cheeks. "We're monitoring dozens of houses and properties belonging to various Russian gangsters."

"And?"

"And nothing, so far."

Reznick shrugged. "Nothing so far. Those are his words, not mine. You've got the best guys in the FBI working on this, and we have nothing. Now I appreciate this is not an easy operation. In fact, it's almost goddamn impossible, against criminal degenerates who are so highly resourced. But the only way of getting any semblance of a breakthrough is to get down and dirty. And if you guys can't do it, subcontract it out."

"We've already got the CIA and Homeland Security plugged into this."

"That's a start. But you need to go further. I'm talking about using the services of a private military company. People that get things done that the government can't or won't contemplate. And perhaps they might—I stress *might*—get lucky. As it stands, the only way we're going to get close to finding Meyerstein is to get our hands dirty."

No one said anything for a few moments as they mulled over Reznick's words.

Stamper shook his head. "Not an option, Jon. We do things our way. No matter the temptation, we do the right thing, the right way."

"And that's it?"

"We're working ourselves to the bone over this. We *will* find her."

"And if you don't?"

Stamper stared at him in deafening silence.

Twenty-Four

Andrej Dragović's cell phone rang as he sat in a late-night diner in Tijuana.

"You leave fifteen minutes after the pickup truck arrives." The voice had a Russian accent.

Dragović checked his watch, which showed it was 10:30 p.m. "I need more details."

"One of our associates will be dropping it off. Do not, whatever you do, attempt to speak to the man or get into the vehicle until he is out of sight. Got it?"

"Yeah, no problem."

"But allow at least fifteen minutes before you drive off."

"Copy that."

"We've made the initial deposit, just over an hour ago. Did you see that?"

"Yes, I did."

"More to follow. A lot more."

"That's what I like to hear."

"We'll be in touch."

The call ended.

Dragović watched and waited and ordered another coffee and slice of pie. Then, at 11:28 precisely, a cherry-red Ram pickup truck pulled up in the parking lot. He drank the rest of his coffee and watched as a tattooed, shaven-headed man sporting a black T-shirt, jeans, and cowboy boots got out. The man lit a cigarette and walked off into the night.

Dragović checked his watch, and kept an eye on the vehicle for the next fifteen minutes. At 11:45, he got up from his seat and left the diner.

He walked over to the vehicle. He opened the driver's door and saw the keys lying on the floor, as promised.

Dragović started up the engine and drove off. He headed onto the freeway, straight for the border. It was the best way for him to enter the States without attracting unwanted attention. He had considered flying straight into JFK. But he knew security there was far more rigorous than in Mexico. Far better to have a long road trip across America than deal with the multiple law enforcement agencies operating at JFK.

He began to slow down. The traffic was at a crawl. He waited patiently, listening to the Hispanic radio channels churning out Latino hip-hop, crazy talk shows, and God knows what else. He swigged some water. And waited. And waited.

Eventually, just before dawn, the vehicle and his fake US papers and passport were checked by heavily armed border police.

"Americano?" said a burly guard, smoking a cigarette and toting a semiautomatic.

Dragović nodded. "Yes sir."

The guard looked long and hard at his ID and passport. Then he was waved through.

He drove on for a few miles until he reached a crummy motel.

Dragović called the number he'd been given. "I'm on American soil." The code words had been spoken.

"Good work." The same Russian voice as before.

Dragović ended the call. He lay down on the motel bed and closed his eyes. He would be up again soon. Then he'd set out on the long drive to New York.

Twenty-Five

It took the best part of six long hours to get court orders signed and for things to get moving. Then they had to wait for another two hours until the Ritz-Carlton's director of security gave the go-ahead for the hotel's surveillance video to be accessed by the FBI. But it wasn't long before they made their breakthrough.

Stamper reassembled the team in the morning. He sighed as he looked around the group of Feds.

"OK, glimmer of hope. We got something. At least that's what I'm being told."

FBI cybersecurity expert Valerie Donaldson opened a folder in front of her. "Surveillance cameras within the hotel show that on eight separate occasions over the last year, Catherine Jacobs visited one suite. The suite was rented by a man named Damian Smith." She picked up the remote control. Up on the screen in front of them appeared the face of a distinguished-looking man wearing a black fedora. "It was rather tricky getting a still image without the hat."

"Deliberate concealment?" Reznick asked.

"We think so."

"Who is this Damian Smith?"

"Very good question. We ran the face of the man on the screen through various recognition software programs, and it brought up the name Yuri Sokolov, who is none other than a junior Russian military attaché at their consulate on East 91st Street."

Reznick leaned back in his seat and whistled.

Donaldson continued: "The consulate is close to Jacobs's office, the Russian Orthodox Cathedral, and the public library."

Stamper scribbled down some notes. "What else do we need to know?"

"The cyber division has been reaching out to agencies across the globe. And we've learned that Jacobs, who we had assumed was British . . . all the paperwork and passport checks show she was in fact born and bred in Russia."

Stamper pinched the bridge of his nose. "You're kidding me."

"No. Catherine Jacobs was born—you're going to love this—Catherine Sokolov in Moscow. She's the military attaché's sister."

"Shit."

"Catherine Sokolov, or Jacobs as she's known, has joint UK and Russian nationality. And we have it on good authority from the Israelis that she may even have been recruited into the Russian secret service, shortly after she began studying at Moscow State University. Apparently Mossad passed this on a couple years back, to someone at Homeland Security."

Stamper shook his head. "She's clearly an agent. The military attaché is an agent. And there's a concrete link between these guys and Merkov. The question is, is the Russian government protecting Merkov and his activities?" Stamper looked across to FBI counterespionage expert James Sanchez. "James, you know more about this stuff than most of us do. What do you reckon?"

Sanchez glanced at his notes before he fixed his gaze on Stamper. "I reckon we got a problem. There are similarities to the deep-cover spying case in 2015 involving a New York banker called Buryakov and Russia's Foreign Intelligence Service. Striking similarities. And I very much agree with Jon Reznick. The woman we know as Catherine

Jacobs, otherwise known as Sokolov, must be a Russian spy. And this doesn't make us look good."

Stamper leaned back in his seat, chewing on the end of a pencil. "Yeah, no kidding."

Sanchez looked up at the screen. "Yuri Sokolov is the product of an old-school KGB family with ties going back to the old Soviet Union. His father was a spy based in Vienna. And he's cut from the same cloth. The sister? We had no idea she even existed."

Stamper's cell phone vibrated on the table. He looked around. "Excuse me, I must take this." He picked up. "Sir, yes, sir . . . Right now?" He nodded. "Very well, sir." He ended the call. "The Director is wanting an update. OK, you know where we are. I suggest we meet up in exactly an hour."

Twenty-Six

FBI Director Bill O'Donoghue was deep in thought. He felt his ulcer begin to burn his stomach. He took a couple of Zantac, and washed them down with a glass of water.

He felt empty. His workaholic tendencies made it feel like he had the weight of the world on his shoulders. His personal life was hanging by a thread. His wife had moved in with her mother in Denver, citing him never being home. But all this paled in comparison to the Meyerstein kidnapping. The advice from Reznick that he should have made the deal hadn't been what he'd expected.

The release of the video by the Russian mob had incensed him. A seething anger bubbled away under his stony exterior. He had authorized the FBI to create a media blackout around the story. And it had worked so far. That was the only success. So far.

His looming congressional appearance was playing on his mind. It should have been a demanding but pretty routine encounter. The politicians would be probing the FBI's response to the terrorism-related investigations. But with Meyerstein not present to answer questions, eyebrows would be raised.

It felt selfish to worry about such matters. But it was inevitable that they would ask why she wasn't sitting in front of the committee, answering questions. He couldn't lie. And if, God forbid, she was killed before the hearing and if it was leaked, he knew he'd be toast. The FBI, an organization he loved and worked tirelessly for, would be seriously damaged.

O'Donoghue headed out of his borrowed office to sit in on a meeting of some of the FBI's finest behavioral analysts and profilers. He listened intently and took notes as they discussed the motivations of the kidnappers, the psychological games they might be playing, and what would be their next move. As they talked, the faces of the special agents were serious and determined.

After an hour, he headed back to his office and called Stamper in. He stood and waited, again looking down on Federal Plaza, the people as small as ants. He wondered how Meyerstein was feeling at that particular moment. He imagined she was alone, helpless. But he also knew she was a resourceful, tough, and intelligent woman who would do whatever it took to withstand such an ordeal.

A knock at the door snapped O'Donoghue out of his thoughts. He turned around.

"Yeah, come in."

The door opened and Roy Stamper walked in. "You wanted to see me, sir?"

"Sit down, Roy."

Stamper did as he was told, getting himself comfortable in the leather chair.

"When was the last time you slept?"

"Couple days, I think."

"You look like shit."

"I feel like shit," Stamper said.

O'Donoghue took a seat behind his desk and leaned back. "I sat in with the behavioral analysts and profilers just now. A lot of really smart people working very hard. But my question to you, Roy, is—are we closer to finding Meyerstein?"

"Not exactly."

Over the next ten minutes, Stamper gave an update on the situation. He outlined the main Russian mobsters among the dozens of gangsters who were under either physical or electronic surveillance. Then he summarized the possible connection to the Russian military attaché and his sister, who was believed to be operating as a cutout.

"We'll obviously have to tread very carefully on this, Roy, with diplomatic protocol involved. I don't have to remind you of that."

"I'm well aware of the sensitivities, sir."

O'Donoghue turned and stared at the Manhattan skyline. "Martha's out there. We've only got thirty-six hours left until their deadline expires. But we still haven't cracked this. We're not even close." He massaged his temples. "Maybe I should spell it out. Homeland Security have intimated that they want their guys to take over, Roy."

"Is this the same Homeland Security who were passed intel on Catherine Jacobs a few years back by the Israelis? Who haven't passed it on to us?"

O'Donoghue sat on the desk. "Reznick said at the outset that we should just hand the fucker over. Realpolitik, so to speak."

Stamper said nothing.

"Martha's life is on the line. We're running out of time, fast. Failure is not an option. And I'm going to tell you, Roy, right here and now, I will do whatever it takes, and I mean whatever it takes, to bring her back."

Twenty-Seven

Merkov arrived by boat on the tiny island. He was greeted by two of his men as he stepped onto dry land.

"How are you, sir?"

Merkov sighed. "Where is she?"

The man cocked his head. "This way."

Merkov and his bodyguards followed him down a path to a shambolic old ruin of a building. The metal gates were flung open and they were shown down a series of corridors, then down a stairwell. They emerged into a room that held the slumped figure of a blindfolded woman, semiconscious, bound by ropes to a chair.

He signaled for his men to move away as he approached.

Merkov pulled up a chair and sat down opposite her. One of his men set a small table beside him, and placed a bottle of single malt on it. He was poured a glass, and he closed his eyes as he smelled the welcome aroma of fine Scotch. He knocked the whisky back in one go, feeling the warmth hit his insides. He put down his tumbler and it was refilled. Again he smelled the drink, and swallowed the lot. He felt good. Putting the glass down on the table he stared at the wretched figure. "This didn't have to go this way, Assistant Director," he said.

Meyerstein didn't move or answer.

Merkov cocked his head in the direction of his men. One stepped forward and slapped Meyerstein hard across the face.

"I said this didn't have to go this way, Assistant Director. A most unpleasant turn of events."

Meyerstein lifted her head.

Merkov sighed deeply. "You don't seem to realize, Assistant Director, that we have the whip in hand now."

Meyerstein spat blood onto the concrete floor.

"You know, Meyerstein, I think under different circumstances we could have been friends."

"I don't as a rule fraternize with murderers and criminals. I put them away."

"Like my son?"

"Yes, like your son."

Merkov felt a stabbing pain in his side from the cancer. "I'm at a loss to understand, Assistant Director, why the FBI are not just cutting a deal with me. It defies any reason. My son goes free and we're able to continue on our way."

"We don't cut deals."

Merkov smiled. "Don't you? That's not what I've heard. I think it's common knowledge that the American government and the FBI are very adept at cutting deals."

Meyerstein was silent.

Merkov smiled, but inwardly seethed. "You think I'm responsible for my son's indiscretions?"

"I wouldn't call murders and torture indiscretions. But if that's how you rationalize it, fine . . ."

"He's my son. I still love him."

"Your son had a very privileged upbringing. You gave him everything, didn't you?"

"That's very impressive, Assistant Director. You've done your research."

Merkov signaled for his glass to be filled once more. "You seem to know quite a lot about my family. I have reason to believe that you are still conducting inquiries about myself and my associates."

Meyerstein was silent.

"Do you know how I know?"

"I have a good idea."

"Meyerstein . . . Both of us, we have some things in common."

"That's where you're wrong. We have nothing in common."

"Oh, but we do. I wanted the best for my son, just like you want the best for your children. I believe you send your children to an elite DC day school."

Meyerstein gritted her teeth and struggled against the restraints.

"How do I know that?" Merkov shrugged. "I know a lot of things. But don't worry, I've been told that they've been moved."

Meyerstein began to sob.

"I think I hit a raw nerve there, didn't I?"

"There will already be a protective detail around them a mile deep. You'll never even get close."

"Perhaps. My son has served quite a few months behind bars. I think he's paid the price. Now it's time to come to an understanding. The problem is . . . no one in the FBI has been in touch with us. They don't seem in the least bit bothered if you live or die." He looked at his watch. "They haven't got long before we dispose of you."

"Is there a point to all this?"

Merkov leaned forward. "I haven't got long to live. Maybe a year. I've been to see the best doctors in Switzerland, LA, London . . . And they all say the same thing." Merkov felt another sharp pain and winced. "Morphine and whisky are keeping me going. Not a bad combination, if you ever get the chance."

"What exactly do you want?"

Merkov slowly got to his feet. He stared down at the pitiful figure, blindfolded and trussed up. "I've told you. I just want to see my son again."

Meyerstein said nothing.

"I'm sorry it's come to this. Really I am."

He turned and nodded to his bodyguards.

A man walked up to Meyerstein and pulled a gun. He pointed it at her right knee. Then he pulled the trigger. An explosion of pain tore into her leg. She began to scream as waves of pain threatened to overwhelm her.

Merkov said, "We will send another video. And another. Until we get what we want."

As Meyerstein went into shock, she felt herself be sick. Lights exploded in her head.

"Scream as much as you like. No one can hear you."

Twenty-Eight

Reznick was checking surveillance footage of the Russian military attaché, Colonel Yuri Sokolov, when Stamper motioned him over.

"Jon, you wanna get some fresh air?"

Reznick nodded, and they took the elevator and headed out onto Federal Plaza, where they picked up coffees from a vending cart.

Stamper found a bench and sat down, grimacing hard.

"You OK?"

"Pains in my chest, nothing to worry about."

"You sure? You don't look too good."

"I'll be fine. Probably indigestion."

"Take it easy, Roy. We'll find her."

Reznick took a seat beside him and was grateful to get some fresh coffee inside him. He looked at Stamper's gray face. He saw a man who was being consumed by the investigation. The false lead that had led them to the Italian mafia must have been a major blow for Stamper. But he had moved on, no longer smarting, and was driving himself and his team to the very limit in the hope of getting a break to get his boss back.

Stamper turned and gave a wan smile. "I hope so. This is taking its toll on not only me, but every Fed."

"We *will* find her."

Stamper nodded but remained silent.

It was difficult for Reznick not to feel a grudging respect for Roy Stamper.

"I wonder if we need to look closely at how we can put pressure on the Sokolovs," Reznick said.

"I have half a dozen analysts looking at that. But Yuri Sokolov's diplomatic status is hugely problematic, Jon."

"I don't doubt it."

"Diplomatic immunity is not something to be messed around with. There are serious protocols." He sighed. "Sure, we could bring him in. But that would blow the whole thing. And Merkov, once he got wind of this, would have Martha moved. Guaranteed."

They binned the Styrofoam cups, walked around the block, and went over everything they were thinking about the case. The fate of Meyerstein. The motivation for her kidnapping. The Russian connection.

Twenty minutes later, they were done talking.

They headed back into the building and took the elevator back up to the twenty-third floor. They went to a briefing room, Stamper shutting the door behind him.

Reznick felt a terrible emptiness. It wasn't just about Meyerstein's kidnapping—it was about the gaping hole in his heart. He saw the Freedom Tower gleaming, only a fifteen-minute walk away. It was hard to believe his wife had died like thousands of other innocents on 9/11. He usually pushed these thoughts to the darkest recesses of his mind. But being in New York always dredged up memories. Her face in his mind's eye. He could still see that smile. If he closed his eyes he could hear her laugh. It was still with him. Deep within him after all these years.

"Talk to me, Jon. You've gone all quiet on me. What are you thinking?"

Reznick turned around. "Do you honestly want me to answer that?"

"Goddamn, yes."

"We need to break some rules."

"That's not how we work."

"I feel like we're going around in circles, Roy. Do you want a chance of getting her back alive?"

"Of course I want to. We all do."

"Then let me speak to the Director. One on one."

"The Director . . . What the hell for? You've spoken to him twice already."

"Look, I just wanna talk to him."

"And if I say no?"

"Then I walk. Out of here. For good. Your call, Roy."

Stamper bowed his head and blew out his cheeks. "Oh, gimme a break, Jon. I don't need this aggravation in my life just now."

"You need to make the call. Either I get to speak to the Director again, or I walk. Right here, right now."

Stamper closed his eyes for a few moments. "What do you think that will achieve?"

"I'm hoping he'll listen to me this time. That's all."

Stamper stood in silent contemplation.

"Your call, Roy."

Stamper sighed. "I need to know why you want to speak to him again."

"I'll tell you why. We're getting nowhere, fast. And sometimes it's time for a high-risk strategy."

"And you think that time is now?"

"Roy, listen to me. If we don't take a chance, she'll come back in a body bag, of that I'm sure. Do you want that on your conscience—that you never went that extra mile for Martha Meyerstein? Do you want to explain at some goddamn inquiry into this whole mess that you denied me the opportunity to put a plan to the Director? Is that what you really want?"

Stamper stared at Reznick. "No, I don't."

"Then let him know that I want to speak to him, one last time, face to face."

Twenty-Nine

It was nearly twenty minutes of waiting as Reznick was made to sit outside the Director's corner office during a conference call. He heard O'Donoghue giving an update to Homeland Security on the grave situation the FBI faced. He heard the reassurances and sound bites and clichés. Stretching every sinew, working every source, and reaching out to every agency at home and abroad. But it wasn't true.

They weren't stretching every sinew. They were playing by the rules. They were staying within their box of laws, regulations, and protocols. They were hamstrung.

He was frustrated. Every hour, every minute that passed, and the odds of finding Meyerstein alive were receding. His stomach began to knot as he realized that it was possible she was already dead. Maybe the Russian mob had grown weary of waiting. And killed her.

Or maybe they were making that calculation at this very moment. It was possible. And then what?

It occurred to Reznick that he felt the same sense of foreboding as when he'd been waiting to rescue his daughter from the yacht off Key West. He remembered the black anger that had threatened to engulf him. But also the terrible emptiness and sense of hopelessness as he'd contemplated losing Lauren.

Reznick shifted in his seat. He reached into his jacket pocket and popped a Dexedrine into his mouth. He went across to a water cooler and filled a cup up. Then he washed down the pill with the cool water.

He checked his cell phone and saw he'd missed a call from his daughter. He called her back.

"Hey, Lauren," Reznick said. "Was just thinking of you. Everything OK?"

"I'm great, Dad. Just checking in to see how you are."

"You know me, honey."

"That's what worries me. You're not the most sociable type."

"You got me."

"Dad, I worry about you."

"Why?"

"You don't have people to talk to or hang out with. I think you need to get out more."

"Gimme a break. I do all right."

"You drink alone, Dad."

"What about Bill Eastland? I drink with him. He's a good guy."

"He's a certified alcoholic, Dad."

Reznick smiled. "He just likes a drink, that's all."

"Whatever. Anyway, I was thinking about coming home for a few days."

"When?"

"In a couple weeks?"

Reznick sensed something was up. "Sounds good."

"There's a guy I'd like to introduce you to."

"A guy . . . You got a boyfriend?"

"Yes, I have. He's nice, Dad."

"He's not got a beard, has he?"

"No beard. Clean-cut. Hard-working. Pretty damn smart."

"What do you say we go out for a drink too?"

"I'd like that. So would Robert."

"Robert? That his name?"

"You'll like him."

Reznick smiled. "I wouldn't count on it." The door opened and the Director stepped out. "Honey, gotta go. Take care. Speak soon."

He ended the call and followed the Director into his temporary office.

"Pull up a seat, Jon," said O'Donoghue.

Reznick did as he was told.

O'Donoghue turned his laptop around. The footage on the screen showed Meyerstein sobbing, blood running down her legs. "They've just kneecapped her."

Reznick watched the rest of the gruesome clip. "Motherfuckers. Is this being analyzed?"

"As we speak."

"When did it come in?"

"Six minutes ago."

"Untraceable, I assume?"

"We're working on it. And so is the NSA. It doesn't look good."

"They're fucking with us. And she's going to bleed out. She's gonna die, make no mistake."

O'Donoghue stared at Reznick carefully. "They're testing our mettle."

"Damn right they are. And that's why I wanted to speak to you," Reznick said. "You should never rule out any options, no matter how difficult it is to swallow."

"Pragmatism I understand," O'Donoghue said. "But this is different."

"Meyerstein is bleeding out in some fucking warehouse. This has escalated pretty quickly. And it will not end well."

"We're all too aware of that, Jon."

"I'm guessing there's no point in bringing Catherine Jacobs in."

"She's tough, if she's Russian secret service. Her cover has been impeccable."

Reznick pondered the issue for a few moments. "I think doing nothing is not an option at this stage."

"Jon, we're not doing nothing. We're using every agency of government from the NSA to the CIA to try and find out where Meyerstein is being held."

"I keep hearing that . . . *We are using every agency*, blah blah blah." O'Donoghue leaned back in his seat.

"Catherine Jacobs, as she likes to call herself, has been networking at some starry receptions. Every party, she seems to be there. Even tagged on Facebook."

O'Donoghue nodded.

"I'm assuming the FBI has some guys scouring social media sites and trying to piece together what we have on her?"

"Yes, we are."

"In what way?"

"I don't follow."

"Are they collating the times and places of receptions?"

"Pretty much. Trying to build up a bigger picture. The photos are from other people who are her Facebook friends. We're also scouring sites using face recognition software, for any Russian mobsters who she may or may not be linked to."

Reznick rubbed his eyes.

"You OK?"

"Tell me . . . Catherine Jacobs's brother, the military attaché—is he holed up at the consulate most of the time?"

"Don't even go there, Jon. We'll have a diplomatic incident. Besides, they wouldn't have sanctioned the kidnapping, but there is a possibility they know where she was taken."

"If I was Merkov, Meyerstein would be moved at least once, probably more. Also, someone within Merkov's inner circle must know exactly what was going on."

O'Donoghue shook his head. "Fuck!"

"Working harder is not going to solve this. Sometimes you need to get down in the shit and get your hands dirty."

"There are plenty of agencies who I'm sure would agree with that logic . . ."

"Sir, I'm not about to get into a discussion about semantics and logic and what dynamics are at work here. I've asked once for you to make the deal. I'm not casting aspersions, but don't allow us to fail just because we were so hung up on technicalities. Pull the strings, make it happen. And get Dimitri Merkov back to his crew and his father."

"There are no guarantees they will adhere to their side of the deal. Dimitri Merkov gets out, we lose every bit of leverage we have to get Martha back."

"I know that. And that's why I want to run a parallel operation to make sure we locate Martha, in case they renege on the deal while we're freeing him."

"A parallel operation?"

"Give me the tools to see what I can do, if releasing him goes south."

"You seem to be forgetting about legal oversight."

"Do you think Martha Meyerstein is worrying about legal oversight? She's wanting us to find her."

O'Donoghue fixed his gaze on Reznick. "This is not what I'm about. Maybe twenty or thirty years ago we might've turned a blind eye to such things."

"Sir, your call. No one need know a thing. I've got a plan in place. I know this sort of stuff."

O'Donoghue went quiet for a few moments, as if he were trying to determine the character of the man in front of him.

"What I can say is that this operation will be under the radar. No one need know. But we need to get this fucker released or Martha Meyerstein will die real quick."

"In the circumstances, I agree. OK, leave it with me."

"There's something else."

"What?"

"I need tools at my disposal for this parallel operation."

"What do you need?"

"I need a million dollars set aside."

"Where am I going to get a million dollars without attracting any attention?"

"I'm sure you'll figure it out, sir."

"What do you need the money for?"

"I want to hire some operatives I know. But they need to be paid."

"What else?"

"I believe Martha is being held in or around New York City. So I need a facility within twenty miles of Manhattan that the FBI can use in emergencies, but which isn't used day-to-day."

"We have that."

"Sir, make this happen. That's all I ask."

"And there are no guarantees?"

Reznick stared at him. "Guarantees are on electrical products. In this line of work, we don't do guarantees."

"Do what you have to do."

Thirty

Martha Meyerstein was floating on a dark lake. She thought she heard her father whispering in the distance. Suddenly she saw her father again. He was standing on the far shore. She could see he was waving. And smiling.

She felt herself drifting toward him. She felt the wind brush through her hair. The smell of pine forests in the air. The aroma of moss and damp grass. She heard a voice like a dark whisper. Her father's voice. *Hang in there, honey.*

She let his words sink in. She took strength from his comforting, familiar voice. Its gruffness only conveyed his certainty and solidity. He was there. He was with her. She stared across the water at the far shore again and glimpsed him once more. He was waving his arms as if to attract her attention. *Not long now, honey. Just dig in.*

That's what he seemed to be saying. She could see him mouthing the words.

She tried to shout, but she couldn't. She was paralyzed. She wanted to shout. To scream. Her father stopped waving his arms. He was looking at her, his eyes filled with tears.

She wanted to shout, "Daddy, don't go!" But all she heard was the sound of the water lapping by her face. She could see him standing there, watching her floating on the water.

Meyerstein felt a sharp slap across her face and she snapped back into the present.

"Look at me!" a harsh Russian voice shouted.

Meyerstein opened her eyes and saw a bug-eyed man staring down at her.

"How does it feel being confined? You feel like a criminal, huh?"

She stared straight at him.

"We will break you. If it's the last thing that we do, we will break you."

Meyerstein smiled through her tears. "Good luck with that."

Thirty-One

Bill O'Donoghue was pacing his New York office, reflecting on the sequence of events, checking his watch. He'd made the call to the Attorney General, requesting the release of Dimitri Merkov. It was well within the deadline. But still no confirmation that Dimitri Merkov's release was going to go through. He'd been told it could be a few hours. Maybe more.

They were running out of time. His ulcer burned as he thought of Martha awaiting her fate. He had never known a case where so little progress had been made. The stakes couldn't have been higher.

He began to envisage scenarios where things went wrong. Where she wasn't handed over. Then he began to imagine what the press would make of it all, if Martha was killed. The flip side would be the outcry if they learned that the FBI had released a convicted murderer into the community. It would be a political nightmare, and one that O'Donoghue was unlikely to make it through unscathed.

He ran a hand through his hair. "Shit."

The truth was he had taken the safe route at first. The bureaucrat's route. The covering-my-ass route. He had made the right call, in a truly legal sense, not to release Dimitri Merkov. But the bold call had also been the right call. Despite the risk of a hostage exchange and the unknown quantity that was Reznick's parallel operation, he was glad he'd made the bold call in the end.

His phone rang. He picked up after the third ring. "O'Donoghue."

"Sir, it's Stamper. I have Martha's ex-husband, Professor James Meyerstein, on the line. I think you should talk to him."

"I'm busy, Roy."

"Sir, I think he needs to talk to you. He's cut up pretty bad about this. He's talking about going to the media."

O'Donoghue checked his watch. He had to prepare for a videoconference in half an hour with the National Security Council. They would want to hear progress. "Put him through."

"Very good, sir."

"FBI Director O'Donoghue speaking. How are you holding up, James?"

"I'm not, if you must know. I keep hoping to get a call saying she's safe and well. But nothing. Days have gone by. I feel like I'm dying."

O'Donoghue took a moment to get his thoughts straight. He didn't think it was a good idea to tell the professor about the footage of his ex-wife. But, then again, what if Merkov leaked the videos to the media?

"James, listen to me. We are doing everything in our power, and then some, to get Martha back. I can't go into details. But please trust me on this." O'Donoghue paused. "James, Roy mentioned you're thinking of going to the press. Is this true?"

"I don't know what to do anymore. I don't even know if she's alive. *Is* she alive?"

Then there was silence on the other end of the line, and in that silence O'Donoghue heard a faint sobbing.

"We believe so."

"Thank God."

O'Donoghue closed his eyes for a moment as his throat tightened. Then he did what he had to do. "James . . . You must speak to no one about this. Because if this gets out, and I'm talking about the media, then we'll lose her. Do you understand?"

Thirty-Two

The next morning, Reznick was in an SUV alongside Joint Terrorism Task Force operative Curt White, headed in the direction of uptown Manhattan. He felt distracted, thinking about the telephone conversation with Lauren. His flesh and blood, his beautiful, smart daughter—out there in the big bad world—and now she had a boyfriend. Fuck.

He began to focus his thoughts back on Meyerstein. A smart, talented, and tough woman who was fighting for her life, every minute closer to death. He remembered she had faced calls for Reznick to be relieved of his involvement with the FBI. She hadn't meekly bowed down to requests from those in the intelligence community who had objected to Reznick. She had fought her corner. And won. He'd seen the steely determination in her cold blue eyes. His mind flashed back to hearing her strong voice coming out of the radio, as the rescuers battled to revive him in a Mexican tunnel.

Reznick knew, at this moment, she would be fighting to survive. He imagined her clenching her teeth, resisting to the end.

"Do you mind explaining what your plan is?" White said. "I mean, where the hell do we begin? Effectively you're trying to lure Catherine Jacobs into our custody, right?"

"That's the plan."

"You mind telling me how you're going to do that?"

"You're Agency, right? Figure it out."

"Back off, Jon, I'm just trying to get a handle of where you are with this."

"We're in the early stages. We begin by getting a team together. And that's what we're doing."

"And O'Donoghue sanctioned this?"

"I'll get someone else if you don't want to be part of it."

"I want to be part of it, all right. So this team you're putting together . . . handpicked?"

"That's the idea."

"New York-based?"

"Yeah."

"How many?"

"I'm waiting on a couple callbacks."

Reznick switched on the iPad he had been given. He scrolled through the limited information they had on Catherine Jacobs. She had slipped under the radar. Most of what they knew about her was from Facebook. She'd posted photos of herself working out at an upscale gym. However, they also had her online calendar, which had been accessed by the NSA. It showed that today she would be going for a lunchtime jog with a friend from her office. Reznick's mind began to formulate a plan.

"OK, I'm thinking out loud, so just bear with me. She's running with a colleague. Central Park. A female."

White nodded but didn't speak for a few moments, as if figuring out the best options. "We could grab both, but that's highly risky."

"We need to peel her away from her coworker."

"Yeah, but how?"

Reznick flicked through Facebook posts of Catherine Jacobs and her fiancé, a square-jawed realtor. Slowly, a germ of an idea began to form. Ideally he would have liked several hours, or days, to plan. But that was a luxury they didn't have.

He pulled out his cell phone and found the number of another CIA guy from the FBI task force who had been assigned to work with him. "Dave, you at the facility?"

"Just arrived. Jon, it's perfect. One-way mirror. Isolated. Couldn't be better. Our tech guy is hooking up the equipment—computers and phones and the rest. We should be up and running within the hour."

"Listen, I need something. I need you to requisition a cop car and two medium-sized uniforms. One for a guy, one for a woman."

"Might be tricky, Jon."

"I'm not interested in knowing if it's tricky or not. Just get them. And don't take no for an answer. I want this stuff to be picked up by one of your guys. And then delivered to the facility, where my two guys should be rolling up any minute. We clear?"

"Yeah, got it."

"Speak soon. We're in traffic. You need to get a move on."

"I got this, Jon. Take care."

Reznick ended the call as they headed onto a tree-lined street on the Upper East Side. "Hang a right and then head up to the bank from there. We can keep an eye on her when she leaves the building."

White braked hard as a dump truck stopped suddenly up ahead. "Goddamn, you fucking asshole."

Reznick peered further down the street. "Take it easy. Four blocks and we're good."

White sighed as they stopped and started in the heavy traffic, which was nearly gridlocked. A few minutes later, they pulled up with a line of sight to the Russian bank's HQ, which was housed in a modernist building. "I'm gonna take a walk around the block, see if there's any better spots than this, OK?" the CIA operative said.

Reznick checked his watch. "Don't be long. She could leave at any time."

Thirty-Three

Brent Schofield was making a mental checklist of everything he had to do as he rode the elevator down to the parking garage. In his hands were briefing papers on terror targets across New York.

"What took you so long, Brent?" the Police Commissioner asked, standing waiting with some flunkies.

Schofield shook his head. "Don't ask."

They were escorted to a black SUV and driven away to a meeting with the Mayor about the latest security threats to the city, in particular Manhattan. His thoughts should have been focused on the various threats from jihadist sympathizers in shitholes in Brooklyn or Staten Island or wherever. But the specter of Max Charles was what concerned him.

He'd known Charles for years during their tenure at the CIA. Charles had been working for the Agency way back when it got its ass kicked by the Church Committee. Charles was among a tight-knit group of extreme patriots who would stop at nothing to further the interests of America, no matter the cost—financially or in terms of lives. Schofield remembered enjoying a nightcap with him at a bar in London, and hearing him talk ominously about "permanent vigilance." Even back then, Charles saw the influence of the Russians everywhere. He viewed communists, communism, socialism, liberals, and social activists as doing the bidding of Moscow.

Max Charles being back in his orbit, albeit as a consultant to the Agency, was a warning sign. Something was afoot. And it was clear that even the kidnapping of an FBI assistant director could be tolerated, if there was a result at the end of it.

Schofield felt uncomfortable if that was the case. He was no bed-wetting liberal, scared of his own shadow. He was a red-blooded American patriot. But the methods the CIA might have been quick to resort to forty years ago should be reserved for regime change in the Middle East only. He had been trained at the Farm, and knew all about assassinations, espionage, and the other methods intelligence agencies the world over deployed. But nothing could justify being privy to the kidnapping of an FBI assistant director. That said, he was loyal to the Agency, as well as to his country. Sometimes, there was method to the CIA's madness.

Schofield recalled the meeting with Curt White and what he'd said about Reznick. The irony was that Reznick was using the same clandestine methods as the CIA to help the FBI get back the esteemed Martha Meyerstein. He reflected on the situation. He understood why there had been a media blackout, and he hadn't even raised it formally within the NYPD. He understood better than anyone what would happen if word got out. He could envisage the headlines in the *New York Daily News*.

It would strike fear into people. Millions would wonder how such a person could be kidnapped and for what purpose. If a senior FBI executive could be abducted and was at risk, the message it would send to America's enemies would be profound. So their hush-hush approach was absolutely justified and smart. But what he couldn't get his head around was their calling in Jon Reznick to join the team. He'd heard about some of Reznick's exploits in the past. A bioterrorism plot on the New York subway that he had single-handedly intercepted. A false flag CIA operation to kill the President that he'd helped avert. Then, two years ago, an Iranian hit squad brought down by Reznick with the help of the FBI.

Some said the guy had a problem with authority. Others that it would cause a scandal if the involvement of a trained American assassin was ever revealed.

The Feds had to know the risks that would entail.

The more he thought of Reznick and the rest of his crew getting entangled with the Russian mob in New York, the more concerned he felt about the asset the CIA had to protect at all costs.

There was a jolt as the SUV went over a pothole, snapping Schofield out of his thoughts.

"So . . ." he said. "Sir, do you want a final run-through of the emerging threats to the city?"

The Police Commissioner shook his head. "I'm good. Tell me, Brent, you really think it's just a matter of time until one of these fuckers gets lucky?"

Schofield checked some papers on his lap. "Absolutely. We don't know when. But we do know one of them *will* get lucky. We can't have our eyes and ears everywhere. We can do what we've been doing since 9/11, getting in their faces, getting in their communities, getting into their communications, but eventually, sadly, all it'll take is one new convert, a lone wolf, someone that's not on our radar, to get through. And it might not be spectacular, but it doesn't have to be. Shooting up a mall, setting off a bomb on the subway, mass shootings in a nightclub like in Orlando, rudimentary pipe bombs in Chelsea and New Jersey . . . You see what I'm saying. The psychological impact to the city would be immense. They know that. And that's why they'll continue to target us."

The Police Commissioner stared out at the streets of Midtown Manhattan. "The problem is the Mayor's people are talking more about inclusion these days."

"We gotta just roll with it. Try and placate those interests, but at the same time, do the work at street level. Use the rakers. Build new eyes and ears on the ground. It's the only way." Schofield's cell phone vibrated in his pocket. "Goddamn, what is it now?"

The Police Commissioner gave a rueful smile as Schofield took out his phone.

"Brent, you OK to talk?" It was Curt White. His heart began to race.

"Not exactly. Make it brief."

"Gotcha." The sound of heavy traffic in the background. "Reznick has his eye on a worker at the Kommerce Bank in uptown Manhattan."

Schofield's stomach knotted. "You're kidding me."

"Sadly, no. She goes by the name Catherine Jacobs. One of those involved in the dead drop."

Schofield knew she wasn't the asset. "If anything changes, I need to know."

He ended the call.

"Who was that?" the Police Commissioner asked. "Anything I should know about?"

Schofield conjured up a lie in a split second. "Just a Langley source giving me a heads-up about a Pakistani jihadist who's surfaced in Brooklyn."

"Goddamn."

Schofield nodded, but his thoughts were already fixated on Reznick.

Thirty-Four

Reznick was sitting in the passenger seat of the SUV, still waiting for the woman known as Catherine Jacobs to leave her office on the Upper East Side.

A burst of static in his earpiece. "Hey, Jon, how's things shaping up at your end?" The voice of Dave, back at the facility.

"Still no sign of our girl. Should have headed out eleven minutes ago. Chatter from her cell phone suggests her friend is at a meeting and running late, and that's why they haven't set off. Tell me, how are you getting on?"

"Just wanted to let you know that our guys are on their way. Crossing the Williamsburg Bridge as we speak. Traffic not great. We estimate you're looking at half an hour ETA. But they will deal with the girl."

"What about the NYPD golf carts they use in Central Park?"

"I have one already in place, waiting for our guys."

"Good work," Reznick said. "What about the translator?"

"The Special Forces girl?"

"Her name's Andrea, if you must know," Reznick said.

"Yeah, whatever, she's all kitted up. Wired for sound."

"She been briefed?"

"We're working on that."

"Don't let me keep you."

Reznick ended the call. He stared up ahead at the building's entrance. A handful of well-heeled people heading in and out. Maybe clients of the bank. Maybe employees taking a break for lunch. But still no sign of Catherine Jacobs. He scanned the iPad, which showed the messages being exchanged between Catherine Jacobs and her friend in real time.

Curt White sighed. "Where do you think these rich fucks swanning around get all their money from?"

"No idea."

"You know what I think? They're laundering their money through shell companies, offshore, Caymans . . . setting up businesses in New Jersey with ill-gotten gains and stolen property, and then shutting it down. That's the way it is."

Reznick didn't answer.

"I mean, who the fuck would bank at some Russian investment bank or whatever in New York?"

"Russian émigrés, I guess."

"Russian gangsters, more like. What's wrong with American banks?"

"They're corrupt like every other financial institution in this country. Bleeding us dry."

"They ain't all bad, Jon."

"Yeah . . . could've fooled me. Let the fuckers go to the wall. They bet on poor people not being able to pay back house loans, and make a killing when the houses are foreclosed. It's gangsterism, pure and simple. We're being had."

"I don't know . . ."

Forty minutes later, down the block, Catherine Jacobs eventually emerged from the bank's foyer with a female friend.

"What've we got here?" Reznick said, binoculars pressed tight to his face. "Yeah, we got a visual. That's her."

White nodded. "Cute."

Reznick watched as Jacobs and her friend did a few stretches on the sidewalk. Then they ran west toward Fifth Avenue. "My guess is they're headed for the park entrance at East 90th Street," he said. He tapped the cell phone-tracking icon on the iPad and it showed their GPS coordinates. He watched their progress for a few minutes and then spoke. "OK, guys, this is for everyone. She's already in the park on East Drive, now headed north."

"We got a visual on her now, Mr. R." The voice of Floyd Chester, ex-Delta Force operator who had been used by the Agency alongside Reznick, years back. Chester was kitted out in jogging gear, a Bluetooth earpiece concealed by his headphones. "Think they're doing a loop of the reservoir. I got them."

"Copy that," Reznick said. "One hundred, no closer. But always maintain visual contact."

"I'm on it, Mr. R. Relax."

Reznick gave a wry smile. He'd lost count of the number of times that Chester had reassured Reznick while they were hunkered down in some shithole safe house in Falluja. *Relax, Mr. R,* he would say. Invariably there would be sniper fire fizzing off the concrete walls of the house. But always Chester would just be chewing his gum, eyes calm. "Just make sure you don't lose them," Reznick said.

White was looking around at everyone who passed. "Sure beats Somalia, right?" He began to laugh. "Man, did you hear what I said? Said it beats—"

"I heard."

"Man, just passing time."

Reznick couldn't abide a lack of focus. He didn't know Curt White and wouldn't have chosen him as his first choice for anything. He was CIA, assigned to the FBI. But there was something about his cocky demeanor that bugged Reznick.

There followed a few awkward minutes of silence. Then Reznick heard Dave's voice, from back at the facility.

"Our intervention guys are now in situ, Jon, about half a mile from you guys."

"Good. What about part two? How is that progressing?"

"Part two is underway. Her realtor boyfriend is playing ball. He's meeting our buyer at some swanky property in Sands Point, overlooking Long Island Sound."

"What about connections between her phone and the boyfriend's?"

"Relax. I've taken care of it. There will be no contact between them while this is ongoing."

"So if he wants to speak to her, even though he's showing some clients around, that wouldn't be possible?"

"Precisely."

"Speak soon."

Thirty-Five

Vladimir Merkov stepped out into the lobby of his penthouse duplex in Tribeca and climbed the stairs to the upper level of the apartment. Floor-to-ceiling windows framed wraparound views of the Hudson and East Rivers, Lower Manhattan, and One World Trade Center.

He went out onto the terrace and sat down on a cushioned wooden seat. Beside him was a table with bottle of Chablis in an ice bucket. One of his men poured him a glass and gave a small nod.

"That will be all just now," Merkov said. "If you can go downstairs and make yourselves at home, I've got some business to attend to."

"Sir." Another nod and the French doors were closed.

Merkov picked up the glass, closed his eyes, and smelled the delicate citrus bouquet. He took a long drink, enjoying the cool alcohol's taste, then put down the glass and lit a Cuban cigar. His gaze took in the New Jersey skyline in the distance.

New York had been his refuge when he'd arrived in the early nineties. He'd be forever grateful. He had become almost a hermit over the last two decades in his attempt to keep out of sight of the FBI. But he loved the bustle. The din. The craziness. He still couldn't help but marvel at how such a chaotic, frenzied, and mad city could function.

Merkov downed the rest of the chilled wine. A few moments later, his cell phone rang. "Yes?"

"I have some news."

"Go on."

"She's lost consciousness. Losing blood. It isn't good. If I'm being honest, she might not make it."

Merkov contemplated his next move. He had nothing to lose. And he sure as hell wouldn't be changing his strategy. If she died, that was their problem. "What about my son?"

"That's the other reason I'm calling."

"Spit it out."

"Dimitri was released ten minutes ago."

Merkov felt elated. "First bit of good news I've heard for a while. Where is he?"

"He's safe. And en route."

"Good."

Merkov had engineered the double cross. He instructed a trusted associate with close links to Russian hackers to get them to send a fake email, on behalf of the Solicitor General to the Department of Justice, confirming Dimitri Merkov should be released with immediate effect as Meyerstein was now at an FBI safe house. He had his son. But they didn't have Meyerstein. It was payback, Moscow-style.

"What do we do when the FBI figure out they've been had?"

"Fuck them. I've got other things to worry about."

Thirty-Six

On the screen of his iPad, Reznick watched Catherine Jacobs jogging around the Central Park Reservoir with her coworker. She wore a gray marl hoodie and matching pants, and pink running shoes. The camera was a bit shaky, as it was attached to Floyd Chester, who was running about a hundred yards behind the pair.

White sighed. "This is taking too long. Where's the NYPD golf cart?"

Reznick spoke into the microphone on his lapel. "Dave, where are our operatives? Are they near the golf cart?"

"Bad traffic. They've just arrived this second at 90th Street. As has the cop car I requisitioned."

"Current status?"

"Our guy is in the police vehicle. And our female operative is just headed off in the cart, up East Drive."

"ETA?"

"From her GPS position and the speed of Catherine Jacobs and her friend, we estimate eight, maybe nine minutes."

"Tell her to get a fucking move on."

"Copy that."

Reznick felt himself beginning to grind his teeth. He had known all the operatives he'd enlisted today for years. The female operative was a Special Forces surveillance expert who was once assigned to Delta Force.

He checked his watch and looked at the iPad. Then he spoke into his lapel microphone. "Chester, you're doing great, buddy. How you feeling?"

"I love to get paid to jog in the park, man!"

Reznick smiled. "Let's try and stay focused. Maybe even just drop back fifty yards or so. We have the GPS of her cell phone."

"Copy that."

The women started putting some serious distance between them and Chester. "Maintain visual at all times," Reznick said. "ETA for the intervention is six, maybe seven minutes."

Reznick turned to White. "You think she'll play ball?"

"Female cop's a nice touch. Less threatening."

Reznick nodded.

"What's the plan if she doesn't play ball?" White asked.

"Let's hope it doesn't come to that."

"But if it does?"

"If it does . . . we'll cross that bridge when we come to it."

Silence for a few minutes, then suddenly Reznick heard a voice in his earpiece. "ETA one minute, max."

"Copy that, Dave."

The situation wasn't ideal. Luring someone on a false pretext in full view of the public posed numerous difficulties and challenges. But as it stood, they didn't have any other choice.

White looked toward the entrance to the bank, farther down the street. "Do you mind me asking why we're parked up here?"

"It's the backup plan."

"Which entails?"

"If she doesn't go willingly, and if circumstances dictate that we can't remove her from the park—which might be difficult if she's with a coworker—she'll come back to the bank. We'll flash our police IDs and tell the coworker we need to speak to Jacobs in private. And when the coworker disappears inside, we tell Jacobs she has to come with us."

"And if she refuses?"

"We put her under arrest. And take her away."

White stared straight ahead and sighed. "You think doing this will get her back?"

"We'll just have to wait and see."

The footage from Chester's camera showed the NYPD golf cart had overtaken Catherine Jacobs. The female operative in the buggy flagged down the two joggers. The images from her own camera were pin-sharp, and Reznick could see Jacobs in high definition, sweat beading on her forehead.

"Which one of you ladies is Catherine Jacobs?" the female operative asked.

"I am," came the reply. "What is it?"

"Ma'am, I'm Officer Janice Mullins from Central Park NYPD. The receptionist at the bank said I'd find you jogging on the East Road about now."

"Is there a problem, officer?"

"Ma'am, do you know a Richard Gruber?"

A look of concern crossed the woman's face. "Yeah, sure. He's my fiancé. Is he OK?"

"Ma'am, we believe he's been in an accident. You might want to come with me. We've got a car waiting to take you downtown."

Jacobs went pale. "Oh my God, is he OK?"

"I can't say any more, ma'am. Details are sketchy. If you want to jump in the back and I'll get you to the hospital."

She stood in stunned silence as her coworker hugged her.

"Catherine," her friend said. "Get to the hospital. Right now!"

Jacobs, looking shocked, hopped in the back of the buggy.

"Ma'am, hold on tight," the operative said, making a sharp U-turn.

A few minutes later, Jacobs was in the back of the requisitioned cop car.

Reznick watched her face. It was etched with concern, tears in her eyes. *So far, so good*, he thought.

"You must be able to tell me where he is?" She stared blankly at the woman dressed as a cop. Then what looked like nasal spray came into view, held by the operative, who squirted it twice into Jacobs's right ear.

Catherine Jacobs's eyes rolled back. Within a few seconds, she was out of it.

Thirty-Seven

Bill O'Donoghue was on a Gulfstream jet headed to Washington, DC, reading a briefing ahead of an emergency meeting with the President's national security advisers, when the phone on his armrest rang.

"Sir." It was Stamper, his voice strained. "We need to talk."

"Roy, this isn't the time."

"Sir, this is critical."

O'Donoghue sighed. "What is it? And make it brief."

"They've sent another clip. It's not good."

"The plan was to have her released by now."

"That's one of the other reasons I'm calling. I'm hearing that the Department of Justice might've just been duped into releasing Dimitri Merkov."

"What?"

Stamper relayed the embarrassing story about the fake email, purporting to come from the Solicitor General, authorizing the Department of Justice to release Dimitri Merkov, claiming Meyerstein had already been released into FBI custody.

"Jesus Christ. This is going from bad to worse. Tell me about this footage."

"It's being analyzed as we speak. Forensics is going over it. But I'll send over the clip."

"So Dimitri Merkov is free and Martha is not?"

"Nightmare, I know."

"Who was overseeing this shambles?"

"We're looking into it, sir."

"Look, I don't think I can stomach any more bad news, Roy. I need to go."

"Sir, there's one final thing."

"What the hell is it now?"

Stamper sighed. "I'm hearing you gave Jon Reznick the go-ahead to run a parallel operation. I only found out about this from, of all people, the CIA operative on the FBI Joint Terrorism Task Force. Tell me I'm wrong."

"Roy, I can't confirm or deny such details at this stage."

"Sir, are you kidding me? I'm heading this investigation and busting my guts, along with hundreds of other agents, to find Martha. And it's OK to keep me in the dark on this?"

"Listen to me and listen good. The limited progress we've made has come from the interventions of Jon Reznick."

"This is ridiculous, sir."

"This whole mess is ridiculous. And you know what? We deserve everything that's thrown at us for failing to find her so far."

He ended the call.

A few seconds later, there was a ping on his iPhone. He tapped the screen and it opened a video of Martha Meyerstein, sitting strapped to a chair, a pool of blood around her.

O'Donoghue felt his throat tighten. Waves of revulsion and anger coursed through his veins. She was one of the most admired among the highest echelons of the FBI.

He watched it again. What he saw was nothing like the woman he knew. The woman who had trailblazed through the ranks of the FBI. Her team was fiercely loyal to her, and she worked them hard. She worked them to the limit. Sometimes she pushed them beyond, for days at a time, to get a result. And she also wasn't averse to sailing close to the wind, most notably by using Jon Reznick during several sensitive investigations.

His mind flashed to Meyerstein's father, the Chicago lawyer he knew from years gone by. A tough, intelligent, no-nonsense man. A man who didn't give an inch in the courtroom. A feared litigator.

She was cut from the same cloth. It was tearing O'Donoghue to pieces to see what had happened to her.

He ran through the possible scenarios in his head one more time. It wasn't just the fact that Meyerstein's life was at grave risk. What was also at stake was the possible leaking of this clip or others to PressTV in Tehran or Russia Today's office in DC, who would be delighted to show this kind of stuff.

It would be a diplomatic disaster for America.

A few minutes later, he saw the lights of DC and the dark waters of the Potomac below.

O'Donoghue knew his fate was tied up with Meyerstein's. Intrinsically linked. He stared at his cell phone. Meyerstein's pathetic, bloodied body, trussed up like some animal. Then he thought of Reznick. He had given Jon Reznick carte blanche to do whatever he thought he could to find her and save her, no questions asked.

Had he damned himself by violating every oath he'd taken as a federal agent?

O'Donoghue closed his eyes for a few moments. He heard his heart beating hard as the engines buzzed in the background. His ears began to pop as they started their final approach.

It was then, as they descended through the darkening Washington sky, that a sense of foreboding washed over him like he'd never felt before.

Thirty-Eight

Reznick stared straight through the one-way mirror and into the beige room made to resemble a hospital room. Inside, an operative wearing a doctor's coat with a stethoscope around his neck hooked up an unconscious Catherine Jacobs to a special drip. Soothing classical music played in the background.

"OK," the operative said. "Time to wake up, Catherine. We think you must have fainted on the way to the hospital."

Jacobs didn't stir.

"OK, Catherine, you feeling better now?" Louder now.

Her eyelids flickered and gradually she blinked in the harsh light. "What's going on?"

"Just relax. You fainted, that's all."

Jacobs tried to lift her head, but groaned and let it fall back on the pillow. "I don't feel too good."

"You banged your head when you fell. Do you remember that?"

Jacobs looked at the tubes in her arm. "What's this for?"

"This is to make sure you're properly hydrated, but it's also to make sure you're relaxed."

Her eyelids were heavy. "I don't want to be relaxed. I want to see him . . ."

"Him? Who's him, Catherine?"

Reznick checked his watch. The drug—a psychotropic known as SP-17—was being administered at a high dosage. But it would take the best part of twenty minutes to take full effect.

He watched as the operative took Jacobs's pulse and checked her pupils with a penlight. "I think you're a bit concussed."

"What happened?"

"You fell as you got out of the police car. Don't you remember that?"

"No. What fall? Where am I?"

"You're in the hospital."

"I can't remember a thing."

The minutes passed as Jacobs drifted into a drugged state. Reznick checked the paperwork in front of him—her health records and biographical history—which had been compiled by Dave.

"Can I get you a glass of water, perhaps?" the operative dressed as a doctor asked.

"How long am I going to be here?"

"Not long. We'll keep you in for about an hour, just for observation, and then we can let you be on your way. How does that sound?"

"My head feels funny . . . fuzzy, if you know what I mean."

"That's perfectly natural."

"Are you going to do a CT scan?"

"We've done that already, don't you remember?"

"No, I don't. Already? How weird . . ."

"Yeah, results are being analyzed in the next room, just to be on the safe side."

Jacobs moaned softly. "The safe side . . ."

"How are you feeling now?"

"Like I'm drifting away. This stuff is good." She smiled.

"It'll help you relax, that's all."

"What?" Jacobs said drowsily. "Where is he?"

"Where's who?"

Reznick whispered into his lapel mic: "When she's fully under, then we can begin the questions."

Thirty-Nine

Andrej Dragović drove over into New Mexico and stopped off at a small motel, showered, and put on a fresh set of clothes. Then he went to a diner close by.

He ate pancakes and waffles smothered in maple syrup, washing them down with three black coffees. Feeling better, he filled the vehicle up with gas and drove due east to Texas.

The miles were long and hard, the sun unrelenting.

Dragović turned up the air conditioning to max and felt the cool air on his skin. He had already been given the route. It was Oklahoma, Missouri, Illinois, Indiana, Ohio, Pennsylvania, and then on to New York.

It was a long, long journey.

He had taken the maximum dose of a stimulant to help him drive more or less non-stop. He felt hyper-alert and sharp. Not an ounce of tiredness.

His cell phone rang. He expected at this stage of the operation to hear a familiar voice. But it wasn't.

"You are making very good progress, my friend." The voice was Russian.

"I was told I'd be speaking to . . ." He hesitated to use his name. "Where's the usual guy I speak to?"

"He is indisposed just now. But he'll be in touch nearer the time."

"He's the one I do business with. The only one I do business with. I trust him."

"Do not worry. He sends his regards."

"But he needs to sign off on the delivery payment, doesn't he?"

"Yes, he does. And he will be speaking to you the next time you hear from us."

"Why the hitch?"

"As I said, he will be in touch. He's just taking care of some business."

Dragović sensed he wasn't being told the full story.

"Any problems so far?"

"No problems. Border was fine. I'm on schedule."

"That is all we want to know."

Forty

When the twenty minutes were up, Reznick spoke into his lapel mic, staring through the one-way mirror at the hastily assembled replica hospital room. "OK, I think we can see she's sedated but still conscious. Let's get going. And let's establish some facts to see if she's telling the truth or not."

The operative disguised as a doctor nodded. "Catherine, can you hear me?"

"I can hear you."

"How do you feel now?"

"I feel good. Happy."

"Well, that's good to know. OK, a few minutes ago you asked, 'Where is he?' Do you mind me asking who *he* is? Is there someone we need to speak to? A relative, perhaps?"

"*Him* . . . you know. My fiancé."

"Your fiancé? Wow! Congratulations. I didn't realize you were engaged."

"Sure."

"Do you mind me asking something, Catherine? Just so we've got all our records up to date."

"Not at all. I'm wide open!" Jacobs began to laugh.

"That's great you're feeling a bit better. I need to know if you're allergic to any medications or foods."

"Let me think . . ."

Reznick checked Jacobs's health records again. He flipped over some pages. "Ask her if she's OK with antibiotics."

"Catherine, are you allergic to any antibiotics?"

"Yeah, penicillin. Bit of a bummer if you contract an STD, right?" She laughed again.

The operative looked through the glass and smiled, before turning his attention back to Jacobs. "Tell me, Catherine, I need to know the last time you were admitted to hospital."

"That would be on my tenth birthday."

Reznick stared at the health records, which confirmed this exact same fact. Catherine Sokolov, as she was then known, had been admitted to a Moscow military hospital with pneumonia on her tenth birthday. "She's telling the truth," he whispered. "It's working. We need more. Ask her . . . ask her if she knows a man by the name of Merkov."

The operative repeated the question.

Jacobs scrunched up her face, as if she were a child deep in thought. "I know of them. The Merkovs, I mean."

Reznick whispered into his lapel mic: "Ask her if they are related in any way, and if the hospital can call them to let them know that she's OK."

"Let me think," Jacobs said after the operative repeated the question. "I just know what they do. My brother does business with them."

"Your brother, thanks. Catherine, we're getting our records up to date. How do you spell your brother's name?"

"Y-U-R-I. Yuri."

"That's great, thank you. And what's his surname?"

"Sokolov, of course."

"So your brother knows Mr. Merkov. Is there anyone else who knows him?"

"My coworker at the bank."

The operative nodded slowly, as if taking the time to pitch the question correctly. She shrugged as she looked through the glass at Reznick, then turned to face Jacobs once more. "Coworker. That's good to know. What's the coworker's name, Catherine?"

"Andrew."

"Andrew . . . ?"

"He knows Merkov. Very well."

"That's great, Catherine. Can you tell me how I can speak to Andrew?"

"Why do you want to speak to him?"

The operative's question grated with Reznick. "Let's drop it down a notch, OK?" he said.

"Sorry, what was that, Catherine?"

"Why do you want to speak to Andrew?"

"I was told he's a good person to know."

"Andrew's the best."

The operative nodded. "So, Andrew at the bank . . . what's his surname?"

"Andrew Sparrow."

"That's great . . . what an interesting name."

Jacobs smiled. "I know, huh?"

"Yeah, interesting name. Guess he must've had a hard time at school, right?"

"No, I don't think so."

"Oh, I'm sorry, I just assumed he'd have a hard time. You know, what with his surname."

"Duh! That's not his real name."

The operative stared knowingly through the glass at Reznick as she held Jacobs's right hand. "Ah . . . that explains it. I should've guessed. What's his real name, if you don't mind me asking?"

"I guess so."

"So are you able to remember his real name?"

"Sure I can. But . . ." Her face scrunched up. "But promise you won't tell?"

"Cross my heart."

"Ivan . . ."

"Ivan. And what's Ivan's real surname?"

"Lermontov. Ivan Lermontov. We both attended the same university."

"That's helpful. And he works at the bank?"

"A private client director."

"Wow . . . A private client director. And he's known as Andrew Sparrow."

"That's right."

"So, if you don't mind me asking, what does the job of private client director entail? Sounds like a top job."

"It's a very important function within the bank. What does it entail? A lot of lunches. A lot of dinners at the fanciest Manhattan restaurants, let me tell you."

"That sounds great. Do you like restaurants, Catherine?"

"Since I moved here I don't ever stay in to cook. What's the point? The best restaurants are here in New York, right? And bars. I love it."

"Do you miss home?"

Jacobs curled her lip. "Not as much as I used to."

"Did you get homesick previously?"

"Yeah, when I was posted to London I was pretty homesick, that's for sure."

Jacobs began to hum a tune.

"I know that song. What is it?" the operative asked.

"Can't you guess?"

"'Stardust.' It's my brother's favorite song. They played it at his wedding four years ago."

"It's a beautiful song."

"Isn't it. My favorite version is by Willie Nelson. What's your favorite version?"

"I think I agree with you. That's the best version. Nat King Cole . . . that was a good one too, right?"

"Oh yeah. What a voice."

Jacobs moaned and closed her eyes. "I love parties."

"Oh yeah, me too," the operative said.

"That's why they sent me."

"What do you mean, Catherine?"

"I mean parties. I'm good at starting up conversations and relationships and becoming integrated into a community or city."

Reznick said, "Ask more about Andrew Sparrow. His interests. His haunts."

"Does Andrew—I mean Ivan—does he head out clubbing with you or visit bars?"

"That's an interesting question."

"How's that?"

"You see, Andrew—and don't be telling people about this—on the surface he's the family guy, the corporate type, the workaholic, and blah blah blah. And yeah, sure, that's him. But he also has his other side."

"You mind telling me about that?"

"Andrew is a fucking sadist at heart. You've got to watch him."

"And how does that manifest itself?"

"I remember once when I was loaded and we were at a corporate function for a client, I was doing some coke in the stall of a bathroom, and when I came out, he was going at it with some girl. I began to laugh and he grabbed me by the throat and squeezed so tight I blacked out. When I came to, he was standing over me. And he threatened to have me killed."

"And this is the private client director we're talking about, right?"

"Absolutely."

"Did he say who would have you killed?"

"He said there was an old Russian guy he knew. And he could get anyone killed, that's what he said."

"What was the old Russian's guy's name?"

"He didn't say."

"Tell me where Andrew likes to hang out . . . when he's not working, that is."

"He likes to swim. Does a hundred lengths before work."

"Where does he swim, if you don't mind me asking?"

"At his home."

"He's got a swimming pool at home? Wow, how cool is that?"

"It's a nice place he's got."

"Have you been there?"

"Sure. It's a converted warehouse in the Meatpacking District."

Forty-One

Brent Schofield was staring out of his window on the thirteenth floor of NYPD headquarters in downtown Manhattan when his cell phone rang. He didn't recognize the number.

"Brent Schofield speaking."

"Brent," a familiar voice whispered.

"Curt, is that you?"

"Yeah."

"You OK?"

"They got his name."

Schofield took a few moments to process the information. "They got whose name? What are you talking about?"

"The asset. I believe they have the name of the asset—Andrew Sparrow. That's what I'm hearing."

"What?"

"Reznick has his name. I swear to God."

Schofield felt himself tense up. "Don't fuck me around, Curt. Is this a joke?"

"Listen, Reznick has it."

"How the hell is that possible?" he hissed.

"Does the name Catherine Jacobs ring a bell?"

"Sure."

Curt White went over everything from the surveillance in the park to Jacobs's abduction to a secret facility. "I'm hearing that she was drugged. Some truth serum the Russians themselves use."

"I know the stuff. And it works. Shit on a stick."

"When she was drugged, she gave the name Andrew Sparrow."

Schofield closed his eyes for a moment. "The fucker is piecing this together."

"It's Reznick, man. Drugged her, and she spilled the beans."

"The name of the goddamn asset? I still can't believe this."

"From what Reznick relayed back to the FBI, she also gave up his real name and address."

Schofield gritted his teeth. The conversation with Charles would be unpleasant.

"Shouldn't we be giving Mr. Charles a heads-up?"

"I'm not sure that's what he would want. I'd imagine if he wants to talk, there's a back channel. Let me think about it."

"How far can I let it go? I'm convinced Reznick is gonna bag the asset and turn the screw."

"How many are on this parallel operation?"

"About a dozen in total, covering different aspects."

"Stick with it . . ."

"You haven't answered my question."

Schofield's mind was racing. "What was that?"

"What happens if Reznick gets his hands on this guy?"

"We'll cross that bridge when we come to it."

Forty-Two

Vladimir Merkov was deep in thought, thinking about the plans he had for his son, when his cell phone beeped. He looked at the de-encrypted message that had appeared. *Got an investment opportunity. Interested?*

These were the code words. And the message meant they had to meet up urgently.

He took a minute to reflect on what Yuri Sokolov wanted. He sensed something was up with him.

Merkov got up and took the elevator down to the underground garage, along with three of his men. He pointed to a black BMW SUV. He got in the back and was driven through the cobbled streets of Tribeca and out of Manhattan. It was about an hour's journey, through the Holland Tunnel and past Jersey City.

Merkov's mind was racing, wondering what had prompted the sudden contact. It wasn't his way to be fearful. But on this journey, he felt a chill right down to his bones.

Sokolov was not to be trifled with. Merkov had met him only once before in person. The meeting was at a beach house on Long Island he had rented for the summer.

He remembered Sokolov cut a suave profile. His suits weren't flashy. A plain navy, single-breasted Italian suit, perhaps off the peg. But it was the eyes. The coldest, bluest eyes he'd ever seen. Sokolov had stared at him for what seemed an eternity before he spoke. They'd conversed in

Russian when alone, and in English when they were with others. The military bearing of the two bodyguards who shadowed Sokolov had been noticeable. Merkov had seen in their eyes the same emptiness he himself possessed. He'd noticed the way they listened when their boss spoke.

Sokolov had been softly spoken, almost a whisper. He remembered Sokolov drank neat Grey Goose vodka. He'd conveyed a sense of power that Merkov rarely saw. It was as if Sokolov, by his impeccable manners, charm, attentiveness, and impressive use of language, made those present understand he was a man to be reckoned with. But also a man to be feared.

They drove due north. When they arrived at their destination, it was dark. Merkov surveyed the leafy street in Montclair. The driver parked twenty yards from the beige, two-story colonial with red shutters. Pink flowers lined the brick path to the front door. A red four-door Honda Civic with an AAA sticker was parked in the driveway.

Merkov put on his shades and pulled on a Yankees baseball cap. The door was opened for him and he climbed out of the car. He took his time walking up to the house. As he approached the front door, he heard the sound of classical piano music. It sounded like Satie, a personal favorite. He pressed the entry buzzer. The door clicked open and he went inside, careful to shut the door behind him.

"In here." The voice of Colonel Yuri Sokolov.

Merkov headed down a smoky hallway into the living room where the music was playing. The curtains were drawn at the front. Sitting in an easy chair, smoking a cigarette and staring out at the lights illuminating the garden pond, was Yuri Sokolov. He wore a charcoal-gray suit and a white shirt with no tie. He pointed to the seat adjacent and Merkov sat down.

"I assume all electronic equipment was left in your car?"

Merkov shifted in his seat. "Yes." He wondered why there were no bodyguards in the room.

Sokolov dragged hard on his cigarette. "We've got a problem."

"What kind of problem?"

"My sister recently did a dead drop for you, am I right?"

Merkov felt a tightness in his chest. "I have no idea."

"You don't know if she was involved?"

"I don't know the logistics of everything. I delegate that to other people."

"I just got back to America late last night. I've been back home doing some work for the government." Sokolov took another drag on his cigarette. "And I was notified that one of my contacts hadn't checked in."

"Meaning?"

"There are people I know. People who I get regular updates from, to confirm that they haven't gone missing, haven't dropped off the grid, haven't disappeared to claim asylum, that kind of thing."

Merkov nodded.

"And here's the thing . . . my sister, who was supposed to send a unique code number to my cell phone at one p.m. today—at one p.m. every day—didn't send that number. I made inquiries. My associate called her office and was told that Catherine had been contacted in the park by a policewoman, who told her that her fiancé was in an accident."

"I see . . ."

"The thing is, it wasn't true. He wasn't in an accident. He was perfectly well, showing a client around a house. I've had that checked out thoroughly."

Merkov nodded.

"Now, I'm a reasonable man. I'm thinking, perhaps it's a mix-up. Perhaps it's someone else. But then I got to thinking *no*, this is not a mix-up."

"What are you saying?"

"Do you want me to spell it out for you?"

Merkov didn't reply.

Sokolov leaned over and crushed out his cigarette in the ashtray. "Do you have any idea what your actions have done? Do you have any clue?"

"I wanted my son back. I need to see him before I die."

"Don't treat me like a fool. I don't believe that's why this has happened. You kidnap an FBI assistant director in order to see your fucking delinquent son? Are you for real? I don't fucking believe you."

Sokolov leaned closer. Merkov could smell the tobacco on his breath. "Did I or did I not authorize such a rash act?"

"You did not," said Merkov.

"So . . . who authorized you to take such action?"

"I did."

A muscle in Sokolov's temple began to throb. "You didn't engineer the kidnapping of an FBI assistant director just to see your son . . . I can look into your eyes and see everything there is to know about Vladimir Merkov. I know you better than you know yourself. Know what I think? Someone has gotten to you. Are there other reasons you need your son on the outside, perhaps?"

Merkov sighed. "That's a fanciful story . . . but I'm a sick man. You know that."

"Cut the crap. We'll talk later about what you're really up to. But in the meantime, let's talk about Catherine. Somehow the FBI has ascertained that Catherine was part of your dead drop crew. They've kidnapped her."

"That's not the Feds' way."

"Well, something seems to have changed. And the Kremlin is not pleased. Does the name Jon Reznick mean anything to you?"

"I have heard that name mentioned."

"We have it from an impeccable source that Reznick has been assigned to the FBI as part of the operation to get Assistant Director Martha Meyerstein back. They have worked together in the past."

"You think this is his doing?"

"Without a doubt. He has Catherine. And he'll be trying to get her to talk."

"She doesn't know where Meyerstein is."

"No. But she knows about Russian operations. Russian operatives. It could very well result in all of them being compromised. And all because you decided unilaterally to try and play hardball with the FBI to get them to free your son. I mean . . . what the fuck were you thinking?"

"Look, I'm a reasonable man, who should perhaps have not been so rash—"

Merkov began to cough hard. He took a handkerchief out of his pocket and coughed into it. He showed the bloody saliva to Sokolov. "I've been told I have less than a year to live. A few days after the diagnosis, I tried to make contact. I was told you weren't due back for another six months. I had an opportunity to take action and no chance to speak to you."

Sokolov stared at him. "You're not telling me the whole story. Getting your son out of jail is for a purpose. A nefarious purpose, am I right?"

Merkov didn't answer.

Sokolov slammed his palm against the arm of his chair. "Do you understand what being a state asset means? Well, do you?"

Merkov remained silent.

"You keep out of sight and pass on useful information, in return for continuing your business."

"And if I don't?"

Sokolov smiled. "Merkov, you need us more than we need you. So, you're going to tell us where Meyerstein is. Right now. And you're going to tell me what the hell you need Dimitri on the outside for."

"Or what?"

"From where I'm standing, you have broken not only our trust, but threatened our strategic interests in this country. And I'm starting to wonder . . ."

"Wonder what?"

"Have you been approached by the CIA—is that it?" Sokolov smiled a terrifying smile. "If you have, all you have to do is be upfront, and we'll sort it out."

Merkov pressed the handkerchief to his mouth and coughed more blood into the white cloth. He wiped his mouth and returned the handkerchief to his pocket. "I knew your mother from way, way back. How is she?"

Sokolov shrugged. "She's not getting around so easy. But she doesn't complain."

Merkov smiled, nodded. "Your father was a better man than me. He used to say I was a degenerate because I stole and I drank too much."

Sokolov's eyes narrowed, but he went quiet, as if thinking of his family back home.

"You were always the bright one, they said. KGB-material, they said."

"Deflection is never a sound strategy with me," Sokolov said. "Release Meyerstein to the Feds, and get Catherine back to me."

"And if I don't hand their agent back?"

"You will die before you can see Dimitri."

Merkov got slowly to his feet. "Leave it with me. Maybe I haven't been thinking straight. I don't know. I'm on medication."

Merkov left the house and shuffled back down the path to the waiting SUV. He slid into the back seat and took a few seconds to compose himself. Then he turned to the man sitting beside him. "I need some business taken care of."

The associate nodded.

"The man inside the house I just visited. His name is Yuri Sokolov."

"Yes . . . ?"

"You will go back in with your brother Nikita. Find out what Sokolov knows about our plans. Be very thorough. Then kill him."

Forty-Three

The headlights of the cars and taxis shone on the cobblestones and converted brick buildings of the Meatpacking District. Reznick checked his watch. It was just after eight. He was ready to go, watching and waiting in a surveillance van with Curt White. He thought they had made a breakthrough getting the name of Ivan Lermontov, also known as Andrew Sparrow. But he knew from his own experience that for every breakthrough, there was inevitably a setback.

Reznick checked his watch again and yawned.

"You OK?" Curt asked.

"I'm good. Sleep-deprived, that's all."

Reznick's cell phone buzzed. He answered after the first ring.

"Jon?" The voice of Bill O'Donoghue.

"Sir, I'm kind of busy," Reznick said.

"They've double-crossed us."

"What?"

O'Donoghue sighed. "The Department of Justice got duped. As did we. Fake email instigated by Russian hackers giving legal authorization for the handover from the Solicitor General."

"You're kidding me."

"Bottom line? Dimitri was handed over. And Martha is nowhere to be seen. We're trying to open up fresh communications with Merkov's people, but the whole thing is fucked."

"How could that happen?"

"Complete mess."

"So they still have her? And he's out?"

"Yup."

Reznick took a few moments to reflect on the information. "Here's the thing . . . why on God's earth would they have gone to such lengths in the first place? Is there a reason they need Martha, other than as leverage? Is she already dead?"

O'Donoghue cleared his throat.

"Maybe the whole bullshit exchange of Dimitri was just a red herring to keep the FBI distracted while Merkov was doing something else right under your nose."

"What the hell are you getting at?" O'Donoghue said.

"I'm just thinking aloud . . . But, really, are we missing something?"

"Like what?"

"Like . . . has this been a setup to get that fucker out on the streets for a very particular reason? What if we've been blindsided?"

"For what purpose?"

"Dimitri Merkov is needed on the outside. There's something in the works. Is that what this is about?"

O'Donoghue sighed. "A couple of our analysts have mentioned this. I think it might be prudent to pull up every picture of Dimitri Merkov from before he was arrested."

"Now we're talking." Reznick saw a top-of-the-range Lexus pull up behind a BMW outside Andrew Sparrow's townhouse. "Gotta go."

He ended the call. Then he watched as a chauffeur stepped out of the Lexus and pressed the video-intercom button twice.

Reznick spoke into his lapel mic. "Car number two, you got a visual on the Lexus?"

"Copy that."

"Slide in, tight as you like behind the Lexus. I'm talking a couple of inches, max. We don't want him out of there."

"We're on it."

Reznick watched as the SUV appeared farther down the street and coolly slid right up to the bumper of the Lexus. "Stand by . . ."

The chauffeur turned back to his vehicle and saw he was boxed in. He approached the SUV, arms outstretched as if annoyed at the stupidity of the driver. "Hey man," the chauffeur could be heard saying. "You need to move."

A female operative stepped out and started remonstrating with him in Urdu. Reznick had known her for years. She was a language specialist, and was also a tech expert who had been assigned to a CIA mission in Pakistan. She now lived in Brooklyn.

The chauffeur raised his palms, as if trying to show he was no threat to her. "Ma'am, I have no idea what you're saying. I was just asking you to back the hell up! I cannot move. And if my boss comes out and he can't make his business dinner uptown, he's gonna be pissed, that's all I'm going to say."

The operative continued to blast him with Urdu expletives.

Reznick wondered when they should move. He hadn't anticipated any chauffeur. He had expected to gain entry and deal with matters inside. He looked around. No one in sight. The rumble of traffic on a busy street further away. He turned to White. "Let's do this. I'll do the talking."

They stepped out of the surveillance vehicle and walked toward the commotion.

The chauffeur turned and stared at Reznick. "Who are you?"

Reznick showed him a fake FBI ID. "You're under arrest. Turn around."

The man gaped. "What the hell you talking about?"

Reznick spun the guy around and pulled his arms tight behind his back. Then he put a pair of plastic handcuffs on him. "Go with my colleague," he said, indicating White.

"You're joking."

White hustled the guy toward the open rear door of the Lexus. The female operative slid in beside him.

"No idea what this is all about," the chauffeur said.

White slammed the door shut.

A few seconds later, the front door to the townhouse opened and Andrew Sparrow walked out. His hair glistened under the street lights as if he'd just showered. Reznick walked straight up to him and flashed the fake ID. "Andrew Sparrow?"

"Yes, what's this?"

"You're under arrest. You don't have to say anything—"

"For what?"

"Securities fraud."

"Bullshit."

Reznick grabbed the man's thick wrists and placed him in metal cuffs, hands in front of him.

"You have no idea what you're doing . . . This is ridiculous."

Reznick frog-marched Sparrow to the surveillance van and pushed him into the back seat as White followed close behind. He was strapped in, Reznick slammed the door shut, and they drove off.

"I want to see my lawyer," Sparrow said.

"Not a problem."

"I want to call him right now."

Reznick turned around and stared at the guy. "I said not a problem. Once we arrive at the office, you can call your lawyer."

"You don't look like a Fed."

Reznick ignored him.

They drove through the Brooklyn–Battery Tunnel and into Red Hook. Past the abandoned warehouses and cobbled streets near the docks.

A huge floodlit building loomed over them.

Reznick stepped out and opened the door to the handcuffed passenger. He grabbed him by the arm. "You mind stepping out, Mr. Sparrow?"

"What the hell is this? This isn't the goddamn FBI."

"It's a satellite office. Get a move on."

Sparrow shook his head. "I'm not moving. I want to see my lawyer."

"Not an option, buddy. You either come with us or . . ."

"Or what?"

Reznick pressed the gun to the man's temple. "Or I'll blow your brains out right here, you motherfucker!"

Sparrow stared at Reznick. "You're not the FBI, are you?"

Reznick turned to White. "Wait here. Keep the engine running. I'm going to deal with him."

White nodded.

Reznick grabbed Sparrow by the collar and hustled him toward some padlocked metal gates. He kicked them open and pulled Sparrow up some steps to a weed-strewn, deserted loading bay. Then through a metal door.

The abandoned grain refinery was perfect. Out of sight. Out of mind.

"Do you know who you're dealing with?" Sparrow said. "You're making a monumental mistake, trust me."

"Is that right?"

"You have no idea, my friend, what kind of shit you're getting yourself into. No idea."

Reznick pushed him up a flight of rickety stairs.

Sparrow spun around and aimed a kick at Reznick's head. Reznick ducked and smashed him in the neck with his fist. The man fell to the ground, semiconscious.

Reznick dragged him up a further two flights of stairs until they were at the top of the refinery. And then through some more metal doors. Then he hauled him to the edge of what looked like an open manhole cover. "This is perfect."

He tied up Sparrow's feet with nylon rope, and then looped another knot over an exposed steel joist five yards away so he couldn't escape.

Reznick slapped him fully awake and sat him on the concrete floor.

Sparrow spat in Reznick's face.

"Fuck you! Who the hell do you think you're dealing with? Do you think you can strong-arm me? You really think that's possible?"

Reznick wiped the spittle off with the sleeve of his jacket, grabbed him by the neck, and squeezed tight. "OK, loudmouth, here's what's going to happen. We are somewhere in Brooklyn, at a disused fucking site with no one around. You scream, no one hears. Now, I'm going to ask you some questions. And if you don't give me some honest answers, we're going to drop you head first down that grain silo."

Sparrow struggled against the ropes. "You know nothing about me, you motherfucker!"

"Actually, Andrew . . . Or should I call you Ivan? Ivan Lermontov, private client director, huh?"

The man glared at him.

"Now, here's the thing. I don't give a shit about the spying operation you're engaged in. And I don't give a shit if you're covert FSB on a slow-burn operation in the United States, trying to forge networks of possible informers for Russia. What I am interested in is Mr. Merkov."

"Look, my name is Andrew Sparrow and I work in investment strategies, risk management, that kind of thing."

Reznick slapped him hard across the face. "Do not fuck with me."

Sparrow looked at him defiantly.

Reznick undid the rope from the steel joist and dragged him across the ground until the back of his head was over the grain silo. "All that's standing between you and your maker is me."

"What the fuck are you doing?"

Reznick began to lower Sparrow down the silo, head first, letting the rope go every few seconds before gripping it again to hold the man's weight.

"Pull me up! Are you out of your mind?"

Reznick let out more of the rope and Sparrow dangled in the darkness of the silo.

Then the Russian began to scream.

Forty-Four

Andrej Dragović was headed down the freeway in the Ram pickup truck in rural Illinois. He pulled into a small gas station, filled up the car, and ordered a breakfast of scrambled eggs, toast, and black coffee in the adjacent all-night diner.

The waitress smiled. "You OK, honey? You looked exhausted."

Dragović smiled but kept quiet. His Eastern European accent was something he wasn't too keen to advertise. Besides, his business was not to engage in small talk. He had work to do. He had a very tight schedule to keep.

"You want some fresh coffee?"

Dragović smiled. "Yeah."

"Coming right up."

The waitress returned a few moments later and poured him a fresh mug. "If you need anything else, you just holler, all right?"

"All right."

Dragović waited a minute or so before going to the bathroom. In the first stall, he checked the cistern and saw a small plastic bag inside. It contained a piece of paper. He had instructed his Russian paymasters to do this to ensure the conversation couldn't be tracked. He pulled it out. Written on the paper was a new cell phone number. He washed and dried his hands. Then he made the call.

"Do you ever sleep?" The usual Russian voice.

Dragović smiled. "Tell Dimitri I'm looking forward to speaking to him soon."

"I'll pass that on. He'll be in touch. And he'll be pleased you are on schedule."

"Trust me, I always am. So, are we still on for New York?"

"That's the plan."

"And he's going to call me? Is that going to be before I get to New York? Because you know I can't deliver until I've got the full payment."

"We know. Trust us on this one. You'll be speaking to him very soon."

Forty-Five

Twenty minutes after he'd lowered Sparrow down into the old grain silo, Reznick was satisfied that the Russian was suitably compliant and terrified. He decided to up the ante. He wrapped the rest of the rope around the steel joist, making sure it was secure with a double-loop knot.

He moved to the edge and pulled a knife out of his back pocket. He held it over the top of the silo. "Can you see this?"

"Please! I'm begging you!"

"Now I seem to have your attention."

"What do you want?"

"You will tell me where Assistant Director Martha Meyerstein is being held, or I will cut this rope, so help me God."

"I don't know! I swear on my mother's life, I don't know. I know she's not in good shape, that's all."

Reznick pressed the knife to the rope. "Listen very carefully. I won't ask a third time. Now, we know you have knowledge of her whereabouts. Let us know, and you'll live. But if you don't, you die. Your choice."

The sound of sobbing. "Please! Stop it!"

"OK, you give me no choice." Reznick began to shake the rope. "Ten, nine, eight, seven, six, five, four—"

"I know nothing! Don't you understand?"

"You know something. So you're either going to talk, or I'll cut off one of your ears, you understand? Chances are you'll bleed to death."

"Please, get me out of here! I'll tell you what I know!"

Reznick held the knife in the space and the steel glinted. "If you double-cross me, I will drive you back here myself and throw you down here, are we clear?"

"Yes! Yes!"

Reznick could feel himself sweating as he pulled the man up. Yard by yard. Eventually, he saw the tears in Sparrow's eyes. He bent down and hauled him out of the silo and back onto the concrete floor. The Russian was quivering, sobbing. Reznick pulled back the slide and pointed his gun at Sparrow's head. "Where is she?"

The man was still shaking.

Reznick pressed the gun tight to his temple. "Speak up!"

Sparrow began to hyperventilate.

"Answer, fucker, or you go down—and this time for good!"

"It's . . . it's a creepy place."

"What else?"

"I was taken there by boat. It's an abandoned island. I swear to God. On my mother's life. That's where they have her."

"Location?"

"I think it's near New York."

"Where?"

"Hart Island."

"Hart Island? Never heard of it. Is she alive?"

"I don't know. I mean, I think so."

Reznick pulled him to his feet. He then painstakingly hustled him back down to the ground level of the refinery.

Just then, Curt White emerged from the shadows and pointed a silenced pistol at Reznick's chest.

"What the . . . ?" Reznick said.

White grinned. "He's coming with me, Reznick."

Reznick could see he'd been double-crossed. His Beretta was in his waistband, his knife in his belt. "Quit fooling around."

"Nothing personal, Jon. I kinda like you."

"Curt, you need to think straight. You need to think this through. I've no idea what you think you're playing it."

"It's Agency rules now. We don't answer to anyone. We do our thing."

Reznick was gripping Sparrow by the throat. "You're jeopardizing the operation to get Meyerstein back, you fucking idiot!"

"Whatever. Are you going to hand him over or does this have to get awkward?"

Reznick's mind was racing. He reckoned that if he reached for his gun, Curt would kill him in the blink of an eye. And his knife was in his belt.

Think man, think.

"Nice knowing you, Jon."

White gave him a deathly stare as he pulled the trigger three times. Muffled shots rang out.

Reznick collapsed to the ground as an excruciating pain erupted in his shoulder. He pressed his hand to the wound as blood poured through his fingers and onto the concrete floor.

He looked up and saw that White was grinning.

Forty-Six

A wintry sun was peeking through the wooden blinds in Bill O'Donoghue's temporary office on the twenty-third floor in Lower Manhattan, when the phone rang on his desk.

"Sir . . . sorry to bother you." The voice was his long-serving secretary, Margaret, who had relocated to New York with him. "We have the gentleman from the NYPD to see you now about Jon Reznick."

"Send him in."

The man was shown in. He was in his thirties. He wore a dark-gray suit, white shirt, and navy tie. He walked over to O'Donoghue, leaned over his desk, and shook his hand. "Good of you to see me, sir," he said.

O'Donoghue nodded. "I'm kinda busy. You want to get to the point?"

The man pulled up a seat and sat down. "My name is Brent Schofield. I'm special assistant to the New York City Police Commissioner. I also work with the CIA on various projects. I want to assure you that this matter is being handled with care and attention. But your operation has inadvertently crossed into other sensitive spheres of operation."

O'Donoghue wondered where this was going. "What the hell are you getting at?"

"You haven't heard?"

"Heard what?"

"Jon Reznick was discovered, bleeding and unconscious, by two NYPD cops from the 76th Precinct on the night shift. Four hours ago to be precise."

"Jesus Christ. Where? What happened? Is he alive?"

"The cops were on a routine patrol of an abandoned grain refinery in Red Hook after spotting a padlock had been smashed and the security gates opened."

"Is he alive?"

"Yes. He was taken to a hospital."

O'Donoghue blew out his cheeks.

Schofield allowed a silence to open up for a few moments as if relishing O'Donoghue's discomfort. "I believe from other intelligence agencies that Jon Reznick worked with Assistant Director Meyerstein in the past. And I don't think it's too much of a stretch to assume he's involved in some way in trying to find her."

"Now listen here, son. You don't come walking into my office and start spouting off about what you do and do not know. And I don't want you ever to assume you know what the FBI does. Know this, though. We operate according to the law."

Schofield said, "I never said you didn't, sir."

O'Donoghue felt his heart rate hike up a notch. He wasn't used to being spoken to like that. He could see that Schofield had pieced together what was happening. And he sensed there was something else Schofield knew. "Are you going to get to the point or not?"

"I made sure that this matter has been taken care of. No reference to Reznick."

O'Donoghue sighed. "What else do you know?"

"He was working with a guy called Curt White, who had been assigned to an FBI Joint Terrorism Task Force."

O'Donoghue said nothing.

Schofield narrowed his eyes. "I know how these things work. And I know how these things can go wrong. But it's important we share information, so we know where we stand."

"I'm all for that."

"You might be thinking Curt White has gone rogue . . ."

"What the hell are you talking about?" O'Donoghue said.

"Jon Reznick was shot three times by Curt White, just so you know."

"What did you say?"

Schofield shifted in his seat. "I know what went down."

"I don't think you do."

"Sir, trust me, I know."

O'Donoghue felt uncomfortable even talking to Schofield. "And how were you able to establish this as fact? Curt hasn't made contact with us."

"He has, however, made contact with me. I've spoken to him."

"You've spoken to him? You say Curt White shot Jon Reznick and you spoke to him? What the hell are you talking about, Schofield?"

"Thirty minutes ago, I spoke to him."

O'Donoghue stared at Schofield. "Now wait a goddamn minute, he's assigned to the FBI. He speaks to us if he's going to speak."

"Sir, this is complicated."

"Don't give me that CIA *it's complicated* bullshit, son."

"Sir, I can assure you, this is not bullshit."

O'Donoghue shook his head. "We have an assistant director of the FBI missing, kidnapped by—"

"The Russian mob, right?"

O'Donoghue let Schofield's reply sink in. "What?"

"I don't envy you, Director. This is a fuck-up on stilts."

"You don't know the first thing about what we're facing."

"That's where you're wrong. What if I told you there are various strands that have come together? The assistant director's kidnapping, Reznick's involvement, and the kidnapping of a senior employee of a Russian investment bank here in New York."

O'Donoghue sighed. He didn't know anything about the kidnapping of a Russian banker.

He realized the investigation had imploded. It was a mess. A terrible mess. And getting worse.

"I don't think it would be helpful to go into too much detail about how I know and what I can say. Suffice to say, Director, there are competing interests at work here."

"The FBI will not be held accountable for the lack of sharing of intelligence . . . you'll know that unlike some agencies, Mr. Schofield, we do everything possible to share what we know."

Schofield stared at him for a second too long. "Director, you'll know in the world we inhabit, there are certain priorities. Triage, if you like."

"You want to get to the point?"

"Jon Reznick kidnapped an employee of a Russian investment bank. This man is a valuable CIA asset. And he's almost certainly been compromised."

O'Donoghue pinched the bridge of his nose. "The guy from the bank was a CIA asset?"

"He's a double agent. He was turned about five years ago. And he's been delivering some notable insights into Russian operations in America, particularly in the banking sector."

"Where is this CIA asset?"

"He's been taken to a secure facility until we figure this out."

"So tell me this. Did this Russian CIA asset know the whereabouts of the assistant director?"

Schofield sighed. "It's possible . . . but we're still to determine exactly what he knows. He's being interrogated as we speak."

"Damn it, Schofield, if he knows, we need to get that information and help us get Martha Meyerstein back."

"Sir, we're doing everything we can. But I need to be frank. This asset is viewed as one of the CIA's crown jewels. And I've got to say, much as we're desperate to help in any way to get the assistant director back, we've got to look at the big picture."

"Are you fucking with me? Are you saying this fuck takes priority over an FBI assistant director?"

"That's precisely what I'm saying, sir. We cannot and will not jeopardize an operation. He is in effect a sleeper agent, sir. A very, very valuable asset who has been deemed indispensable by the National Security Council, who are aware of his importance."

O'Donoghue couldn't believe what he was hearing. "So I've got an assistant director kidnapped and another guy in hospital. And there's nothing I can do about it?"

"We're working hard to resolve this situation."

O'Donoghue slammed the palm of his hand down on his desk, sending papers flying. "Not a fucking option, son."

"That's where you're wrong. If the Secretary of Homeland Security realized the workings of the FBI in this operation, you'd be indicted before a grand jury, of that I can guarantee you."

Forty-Seven

Reznick was hearing dark whispers. He sensed there were people near him. His mind flashed up fragmented memories. He thought he saw his wife. Then a blinding light.

"Jon . . . can you hear me?" A female voice. "Jon . . . wake up. Wake up, Jon."

Reznick tried to open his eyes but couldn't.

"Jon," the voice said, "it's time to wake up. You're safe."

Reznick slowly managed to open his eyes to the blurred image of a woman in blue.

"Hi," she said. "I'm Dr. Marie Lopez. How are you feeling?"

Reznick squinted as the doctor came into focus. Her brown eyes and gentle smile made him feel good. Then he felt a sickening, burning sensation in his shoulder. "Goddamn . . ."

"I can imagine. We've given you pain relief, so that'll take the edge off. A bullet grazed your shoulder. Severe chest bruising. So my advice is you need to rest up for the next few days."

Reznick's mind went back to Curt White shooting him at the grain refinery in Brooklyn. "Where am I?"

"New York Methodist Hospital. You're in Brooklyn."

"Am I ever going to escape from Brooklyn?"

The doctor laughed. "I think that very same thought each and every day, trust me."

Reznick stared at her as he tried to piece together recent events. "I need a phone."

"A phone?" Dr. Lopez shook her head. "You need to rest. You're strictly in recovery mode."

Reznick looked around the room. "Where are my clothes?"

"Blood soaked from the bullet wound in your shoulder. Thankfully you had the good sense to wear an FBI bullet-resistant vest."

"At least I got something right, huh?"

Dr. Lopez smiled. "You lost some blood. But we got the slug out of your shoulder. Trust me, you were lucky."

Reznick winced as he felt a burning pain in his shoulder. He began to scrunch up his eyes. "Can you up the morphine, Doc?"

"Can do."

"Have you got the things in my possession. Cell phone, wallet and stuff?"

The doctor pointed to the small bedside table. "Bottom drawer, it's all there in a Ziploc bag."

"Thank you."

"How long have I been here for?"

"You were brought in this morning."

"What time is it?"

The doctor looked at her watch. "Nearly one o'clock . . . p.m. I meant to say, there's a man from the FBI wanting to speak to you."

"Where?"

"He's outside."

"What's his name?"

"Stamper. Ring a bell?"

"Send him in, Doc."

The doctor smiled and left the room. A few moments later, Stamper was in front of him. He was carrying a garment bag and a small black overnight bag. "Jesus Christ, Jon. What the hell?"

"Yeah, nice to see you too, Roy."

Stamper pulled up a chair and sat down beside Reznick, placing the bags on the bed. "Man, I'm so sorry . . . I wish to God . . ." His voice trailed off.

Reznick edged himself upright. He moaned as the pain shot through his shoulder.

"You OK?"

"Of course I'm not OK, Roy. What the fuck is wrong with you?"

"Sorry . . ."

"Roy, look, we haven't got much time."

"Jon, you should've kept me in the loop. This is a mess. This is what happens—"

"I haven't got the time or energy for lectures or to argue with you. First of all, what's the latest, apart from me getting shot?"

"Well, the investigation has gotten a lot more complicated. Thanks in part to you kidnapping the Russian banker. This is a CIA thing now . . . the guy you got your hands on, the banker, he's a double agent . . . the Agency turned him."

"That figures. Roy, there's more to this. We're still missing something. Dimitri is needed on the outside, of that I'm sure. We need to join up the dots."

Stamper nodded. "Homeland Security is going nuts. And so is the National Security Council. They're saying Sparrow is to be protected at all costs."

"I don't answer to Homeland Security or the National Security Council. I don't answer to anyone."

"Jon, let's not go there . . . We need to back up. Now is not the time to go out on a limb again."

"Now is exactly the time to go out on a limb!" Reznick tapped the side of his head. "Besides, it's all in here."

"What is?"

"Andrew Sparrow . . ."

"Ivan Lermontov, you mean?"

"Yeah . . . he gave me something."

"He gave you what?"

"He told me about a trip to Hart Island he made. Where the hell is that?"

Stamper scrunched up his face in thought. "I think that's in Long Island Sound."

"We need to go there."

"Absolutely. We'll check it out." Stamper pointed at the bags on the bed. "Got a change of clothes for you when you get out. In the meantime, just rest up."

"Not a chance. I'm going with you."

"You're kidding me."

"Do I look like I'm fucking kidding? Let's get to this, right now."

Forty-Eight

The cab dropped Brent Schofield off at the Fifth Avenue entrance to a private gated street, Washington Mews, in the heart of Greenwich Village. He walked halfway down, to a beautiful stucco-fronted town-house with a gray door. It was a CIA safe house. He pressed the buzzer and was let in. He walked up the stairs to a lobby area, where Curt White was sitting with the CIA asset, Andrew Sparrow.

He stared down at Sparrow. "How you feeling now?"

"I'm OK, thank you."

"My first concern is that your cover is maintained."

Sparrow shrugged. "You want me back at the bank?"

"You must maintain your cover."

"I missed a scheduled call from my handler."

"You just say you dropped your phone in your car and didn't notice until later."

"They're not stupid people."

Schofield sighed. "I'm well aware of that."

"I don't want to go through that again. I think my cover has been blown, well and truly."

"Let's not be too hasty." Schofield's cell phone rang. He saw the caller ID and left the room, shutting the door behind him. "Sir, how are you?"

"Where the hell are you?" The voice of Frank Calhoun, New York City Police Commissioner.

"Sir, I'm with a contact of mine in the Village. What's the problem?"

"Haven't you heard the news?"

"Like I said, I'm meeting a contact."

"Listen to me. The shit is about to hit the fan."

"How come?"

"A Russian military attaché, Sokolov, has just been found dead. Out in New Jersey."

"You can't be serious," Schofield said.

"Question is, what the hell would this be about? This is way out of left field. I mean, what the hell was he even doing out there?"

"We need to talk about this. About the response."

"I'm chairing a meeting. In my office, one hour."

"You got it."

The line went dead.

Schofield punched in the number for Max Charles, his ex-CIA mentor. Three rings and he picked up.

"Brent, talk to me."

"Sir . . . we've got a bit of a situation developing."

"I'm listening."

"A Russian military attaché, Sokolov, has just been found dead."

"You better be fucking with me, Brent."

"Sir, this is no joke. I just got the news from the New York Police Commissioner, no less."

"You thinking what I'm thinking?"

"It's clearly blowback from Merkov . . . Linked to this whole shit-storm. We know Merkov and Sokolov go way back. That crazy fuck Merkov has lost his mind, that's for sure."

"Sparrow is our main concern. Keep him safe. He's still got a part to play."

"Don't worry about him. My problem is that I've been ordered back to base for an emergency meeting about the response to this."

"What does the FBI know?"

"They know we have the asset, Andrew Sparrow. And we're calling the shots. But they don't know the endgame."

"So far. What did they say?"

"They weren't too pleased, let me tell you."

"No kidding. OK, let's establish the facts. How is he?"

"Sparrow is safe and well, sir. Bit shaken up. I just arrived a few minutes ago."

"We have a limited window of opportunity. Sparrow is Merkov's banker."

"I know. Sparrow knows everything about his wealth. But he also knows all about the thousands of companies in the Caymans, Switzerland, and Panama where Merkov directs money from the Russian mob and the Russian government."

"You're missing something. Sparrow is only one part of the equation. Bottom line? There's only one person who's authorized to transfer money from any of these accounts."

Schofield took a few moments to contemplate what he was being told. "Dimitri Merkov?"

"Clever boy. For the operation to go ahead, we need him in person. That was the plan, and it was straightforward eighteen months ago when we started this."

"But Dimitri Merkov's incarceration kiboshed that?"

"Precisely. We needed him out. He alone can move the funds to our fall guy."

Schofield was almost immune to the machinations and the Machiavellian mindset of the Agency. But this time he was stunned at the complexity of the operation. "What exactly is the endgame?"

"That's need-to-know. All that's required of you is to get Mr. Sparrow and hook him up with Dimitri Merkov, and get the money into the hands of the group who have been subcontracted to do the hit."

"The hit . . . ?"

"I've said too much. We need Sparrow and Dimitri to transfer the final tranche to the contractor at his Swiss bank account, set up for the operation and other ancillary activities."

Schofield paused to let the information sink in.

"Sir, did I hear you correctly?"

"Sparrow knows the details. But it's Merkov junior who has the biometric approval. He'll then transfer those details to our encrypted cloud storage facility, and get the money moving."

Schofield said nothing as he continued to digest the information.

"Explain the situation to Sparrow. And tell him this is required and we will set him up for life, with a new identity in any place of his choosing in America."

"When do we move on this?"

"You need to do this right now."

"Look, I'm needed downtown by the NYPD, not to mention the Feds will be looking for Curt."

"Don't worry about that. I'll put in a couple calls. Your number-one priority is Andrew Sparrow."

"What about Dimitri Merkov?"

"He's en route to Manhattan. They need to link up within the next hour."

"There's also the situation with Meyerstein."

"Don't worry about that. You've got work to do."

The line went dead.

Schofield contemplated the conversation before he went back into the lobby. Sparrow was sitting quietly as Curt White stared at him. "You can access Merkov's secret offshore accounts?"

"Yes, I can access them. But I need the retinal scan and thumbprint of Dimitri Merkov for money to transfer."

"He's en route."

"I've dealt with him before."

"What's he like?"

"A bastard. But it's business. You learn to live with it. But, sure, we can do that. I'll have to go back to the office."

"Not an option."

"The only other way is for me to use a special laptop."

"Where's that? At your house?"

Sparrow smiled. "Absolutely not. It's in a security box in Chinatown. Dimitri Merkov picked the bank."

"OK, that'll work. What's the name of the bank?"

"Industrial and Commercial Bank of China. Canal Street."

Schofield's cell phone rang.

"Brent?" It was Charles again.

"Sir?"

"Dimitri's people need to know the next move."

"Tell him to meet us inside the Industrial and Commercial Bank of China on Canal Street in one hour's time."

Forty-Nine

Reznick felt himself breathing hard as he sat in the lead FBI chopper headed for Hart Island, two heavily armed SWAT members strapped in beside him. The burning pain in his shoulder was only being kept at bay with morphine tablets, and Dexedrine to work against the sedative effects. In the distance was the island.

He was handed a pair of binoculars and trained them on the strip of land. He carefully surveyed the barren terrain, decrepit buildings open to the elements. They'd been told that Hart Island had once housed a prison. But it was also the final resting place for countless stillborn babies, as well as the poor, homeless, and destitute. As they got closer, he spotted something at the far end of the island.

"North-northwest, you see that?" Reznick said.

The pilot's voice in his headphones: "Can't see anything, Jon."

"Like a small fire. And a few people. Get in close."

The chopper swooped down low for a better look.

Reznick could see some figures beside a pier. "There's a small boat bobbing about, you got it?"

"Copy that," the pilot said.

"Get right above them."

The chopper went directly over them and the people looked up.

Reznick swapped the binoculars for a rifle and trained its scope on the men. "Four of them. Tell them over the loudspeaker to put their hands in the air. FBI."

The pilot issued the warning, and the men complied as the fire was stoked in the downdraft.

Reznick could see the men all had their hands up. The chopper moved to within a hundred yards of the men and landed adjacent to an abandoned building.

He kept the rifle trained on the men. "On your knees! Hands on head! Now!"

The men did as they were told as Reznick approached them.

"Do not fucking move!"

The two SWAT team members fanned out across the island. Then the second chopper landed and the rest of the team stormed out.

Reznick walked up to the guy nearest him and pointed the rifle straight at his head. "Who the hell are you?"

"My name is Leonard Moritz. We're just out fishing."

Reznick looked at the others. He could see frightened regular Joes, not hardened mobsters. "Fishing . . ."

"Yeah," Moritz said. "I got ID. We all work over at Rikers. We're prison guards, man."

Reznick heart sank. "You're joking."

They all shook their heads.

"I want to see Rikers IDs from all of you, nice and slow."

The men very slowly reached into their back pockets and threw their identification at Reznick's feet. He picked them up and checked each of their faces. Then he frisked every one. No guns. Just a fishing knife.

Moritz said, "What the hell is this all about?"

"We believe a woman was brought here and held prisoner."

Moritz looked around at the other guards and they all shrugged. "There's nothing here but us, man. Just abandoned old places on the island."

Reznick motioned for one of the SWAT team to come over. "Search their boat."

The guy did.

"Not a thing, Jon. All clear. Just some fishing gear."

Reznick ordered him to cover the fishermen. "Don't let them out of your sight."

The guy nodded, rifle trained on the frightened men.

Reznick and the rest of the team fanned out and began to search the 131-acre island. He pushed open the rotting door of a building. The stench of rotting animal flesh was in the air. They headed up to a decaying redbrick premises that had been a prison. Crumbling wooden floors creaked under their weight. On and on they searched the island's buildings. Every inch. Every room. Down into dank basements with flashlights. Bats brushed by. Night-vision sights activated as they headed down eerie corridors.

Deeper and deeper into the bleak bowels of the island. Behind thick steel doors. It seemed the ghosts of the past were lingering, as if watching their every move.

Reznick signaled for them to move out. They proceeded to the very tip of the island, down by the shoreline. The old abandoned jetty.

A couple of hours later, when they had covered every possible space on the island, it was clear she wasn't there.

Reznick's earpiece crackled into life, with confirmation from the gruff voice of the SWAT team leader.

"Nothing, Jon," he said. "Goddamn nothing. No sign of life. Just those crazy fucks beside the fire."

"Copy that," Reznick said.

It slowly began to dawn on Reznick that Sparrow had, despite being at death's door, lied to him. Even with a gun to his head, and his head down a grain silo, the fucker had taken him on a wild goose chase.

Reznick headed back down toward the fishermen, who were still being watched by armed men. "Guys, we had the wrong information.

We got it wrong. Hope you aren't offended. We were just chasing down a lead."

Moritz blew out his cheeks. "Man, hey, it happens. We deal with bullshitters every day."

"However, I must caution you. Do not mention this to anyone. Family, friends. And definitely no social media. Any sign of this, we have your names, and you will be in danger of jeopardizing a federal investigation. Do you understand me? We'll come looking for you. We understand each other?"

All the men nodded as one.

Reznick turned and headed back to the chopper.

"Where to?" the pilot asked.

Reznick seethed as he strapped himself in. "Get the hell out of here. What a mess."

Fifty

Brent Schofield was in the back of the SUV with Sparrow by his side when they pulled up outside the bank in Chinatown. His cell phone rang. He didn't recognize the caller ID. "Yeah?"

"Brent Schofield?"

"Speaking. Who's this?"

"Where the hell you been?"

"I'm sorry, who's this?"

"Dimitri, that's who."

Schofield gathered his thoughts. "Of course. Where are you?"

"Bank. Vault. Where the fuck do you think?"

They got out of the car and headed into the bank. A manager was waiting and escorted them down to the strong room.

Dimitri Merkov was sitting, flanked by two bodyguards. He nodded to Sparrow. "OK, let's do this."

Sparrow took two keys from his pocket and opened the safe-deposit box. He reached in and pulled out a backpack. He turned to the banker. "Where's a private room where we can open this?"

The banker punched a code into the keypad outside a door and let them in. Schofield followed Sparrow, Dimitri, and the two bodyguards into the room. There was a table and chair inside. The door clicked shut behind them.

Sparrow put the backpack on the table and sat down. He unzipped the backpack and pulled out a MacBook Pro. He opened it up and switched it on, then keyed in a passcode when prompted.

The window opened up showing hundreds of accounts. Then it switched to a biometric face scanner.

Sparrow got up off the chair.

Dimitri Merkov slumped down in front of the laptop. He stared at the green dot of the computer's camera.

"Stay completely still, Dimitri," said Sparrow.

A click, and Merkov's image appeared on the screen.

"It'll be scanning the iris from the picture, so it'll be a few seconds."

A green tick on the screen.

"We're in business," Sparrow said. "How much do you want transferred?"

"Ten million dollars up front to Mr. Dragović's Geneva account."

Schofield had heard the name a few years back down at the Farm. Dragović was a Serbian hitman who carried out political assassinations. He had worked for the Russian government across Western Europe. Schofield remembered an MI6 contact in London telling him that the only time they knew Dragović had entered the UK was weeks after a Chinese dissident, living in the north of Scotland, had fallen to his death on a cliffside walk. It had emerged, after interviewing some fishermen, that Dragović had entered the country on an Icelandic trawler. But the trail had gone cold by the time MI6 had pieced together the details of the intricate assassination.

Merkov got up from the chair and Sparrow sat down again. He tapped a few keys and turned to look at Dimitri. "Any message you want sent with the money?"

"It's encrypted, right?"

"Military encryption, and then some."

Merkov sighed heavily. "My father sends his love and respect. And a further ten million dollars will be transferred to your Zurich account on delivery."

Sparrow typed in the message and sent it. "So, ten million dollars has been transferred. And a further ten million is pending approval via encryption messaging by myself, upon request."

Dimitri nodded. "Good. Are we done?"

Sparrow logged out and shut down the computer.

Schofield cleared his throat. "We're good. And we're done. The endgame is in play."

Merkov hugged Sparrow and shook Schofield's hand. "I'm going to disappear for a while."

"Very wise."

He put on some shades and left the room with his two bodyguards.

Schofield watched closely as Sparrow put the laptop in the backpack and went out of the room to lock it back in the safe-deposit box.

Sparrow signed himself out and they were escorted out of the building. They got into the back of the SUV, Curt White up front in the passenger seat.

The driver glanced in the rearview mirror. "Where to?"

"Let's head out of the city," Schofield said. "Anywhere."

"You got it."

They pulled away and drove through Lower Manhattan and across the Brooklyn Bridge.

Schofield dialed a number on his cell phone.

"Yes?" The voice of Max Charles.

"First step has been taken."

"Excellent work."

"Have you got any further instructions?"

"I'll call you back in an hour. Head to the safe house in Bridgeport."

Fifty-One

When they got back to the FBI office in Lower Manhattan, Reznick was summoned into the corner office to see O'Donoghue.

He turned around. "You look terrible."

"Yeah, thanks."

O'Donoghue bowed his head and sighed. "What a fuck-up. How you feeling?"

"I'll survive."

"How in God's name did we get in this mess?"

"Curt White double-crossed us. Merkov double-crossed us. We're being fucked over every which way."

"We're using every available intelligence-gathering asset, and we're still falling short. The CIA say they are looking into what happened, but that doesn't mean shit. Martha Meyerstein is not as important to the strategic interests of the United States of America as the man you know as Andrew Sparrow."

"There's more to this than just Meyerstein. I'm sure of it."

"So am I."

"What do you mean?"

O'Donoghue looked drained, mentally exhausted. "The fingerprints of the CIA are already all over this."

Reznick pulled up a chair and slumped down. "Andrew Sparrow is a piece of work. Very smart. He gave me the name of Hart Island. I would have sworn that this information was correct. He was dangling by a fucking rope when he gave me the information."

"They must've moved her."

"I don't get it. I keep on trying to figure out what the hell I did wrong. I really didn't foresee one of our guys shooting me up. Fucker left me for dead."

"We've all made a lot of wrong calls on this one. This whole investigation would have progressed differently if we'd known it intersected with a CIA operation from the start." O'Donoghue sighed. "Homeland Security is busting my balls on this. They're pulling rank, wanting us to take a step back. The FBI will never back off. Not on this. That's not the way we work. But sometimes there's politics involved at this level. You have to suck it up."

"Sounds like there's a lot of interagency bullshit going on."

"You don't know the half of it."

"Try me."

O'Donoghue shook his head. "There's something you need to know. After you were shot, I was visited, in this very office, by someone with the CIA. Works here in New York for the Police Commissioner."

Reznick whistled.

"He explained the asset was of incredible value to this country, and admitted the asset was in the Agency's hands. My understanding is that Andrew Sparrow is a double agent. A Russian, real name Lermontov, working as a banker in New York, now spying for the CIA. But still linked to the Merkovs."

Reznick said nothing.

"It is what it is, he said."

"Hope you told him to go fuck himself."

"It was too late for that, Jon. They had all the cards."

"And then he disappeared?"

O'Donoghue nodded. "Cold as ice."

"Son of a bitch." Reznick's mind was racing. "Compromised from the inside." He kicked over a trash can, the contents of a near-empty Coke can spilling out onto the carpet.

———

Reznick needed to clear his head. He felt they were close. But, in fact, the disappointment of Martha Meyerstein not being on the island was shattering. He headed outside for fresh air and walked a few blocks, doing what he had been trained to do. He began to focus and think about the case. It was clear that Curt White had been operating within the FBI task force for some time. He'd shown his hand to protect the asset and the Agency, no matter the fallout for the FBI.

He began to think about getting back to basics. The first people who had contacted him. Someone who would know more about Martha Meyerstein. He needed to know the smallest details of her working life, her investigations, perhaps a strand of her personal life he wasn't privy to. Something that could have a bearing on what had happened to her. Had she confided her innermost thoughts on what was happening with her team at FBI Headquarters?

Reznick was reluctant to contact Professor Meyerstein. But as it stood, he needed someone to give him something, even a sliver of information.

He pulled up her ex-husband's cell phone number.

"Oh my God, any news?" James Meyerstein asked when he picked up, the tension heavy in his voice.

"Nothing so far, sorry."

Meyerstein groaned. "I can't take this."

"We're doing everything, and I mean everything. James, I'm trying to figure out how Martha viewed her colleagues within the FBI."

"Why would I know that?"

"Well, just you being married to her at one time, if she'd shared any concerns about those who worked for her."

"None at all. But saying that, we've been divorced for several years now."

Reznick sighed. "Was there anyone she confided in about her work?"

"No one. She's always been self-contained." That reminded Reznick of himself. "Saying that, there was one person she did trust and open up to."

"Who's that?"

"Her father."

"Her father . . . Sure . . ." Reznick sighed. "Can you do me a favor?"

"What?"

"I'm going to need to speak to Martha's father. Can you give me his number?"

Meyerstein cleared his throat. "OK. But please, you must promise me, go easy on him." He gave Reznick the number.

"James, I appreciate this."

"Please find her."

"We're doing our utmost, I can assure you. Hang in there."

Reznick hung up, and then called Meyerstein's father.

"Yes?" The voice was solid.

"Sir, you don't know me, my name is Jon Reznick."

A beat. "Martha's mentioned you. Don't tell me bad news, please. It'll be too much."

"Sir, no news. I'm sorry." A silence opened up. "We're busting our guts on this, trust me. I'm sorry for contacting you, sir, but I want to ask a couple questions about Martha and the people around her at the FBI."

"I didn't know them."

"Yes, but did she talk to you about her work at all?"

A deep sigh down the line.

"I'm looking for anything."

"Do you want to be more precise?"

"Sir, did she ever confide in you about concerns regarding those around her at the FBI?"

"Is this connected to her kidnapping?"

"Not directly. Maybe. I don't know. I'm just trying to build a picture. To see if we're missing anything that would give her kidnappers reason to continue holding her. It might be something you maybe don't believe will help us find Martha. But it might help—in other, more indirect ways—to lead us to her. I'm sure you've probably gone over this already with the FBI . . ."

"The Feds haven't gotten us involved at all."

"Not even interviewed you?"

"Not at all. They've closed up shop."

Reznick found that not only strange but troubling. "Sir, back to my point. Had she any concerns about people at her work?"

"Yes."

"Do you mind me asking what kind of concerns she had?"

"The first time . . ."

"The first time?"

"She had no one to talk things over with since her husband left. Sure, she talked things over with her team at the Hoover Building. But . . . the first time was about three years ago. She was heading up a team investigating Vladimir Merkov. You heard of him?"

"Yes, I have."

"That case was causing her concern from the outset. Strange things were happening."

"Like what?"

"Files going missing. Interview notes going missing. And eventually the case against him went south and a decision was made to scrap the investigation."

"Where did she see the root of the problem?"

"She thought it was internal."

"Did she raise these concerns?"

"Yes. And it was referred to the Internal Investigations Section of the FBI. But it just dragged on and on, no resolution or conclusion. No report."

"So they buried it."

"Precisely."

"Tell me about the second time."

"The second time, same as the first in that she talked things over with me. When she went after Dimitri Merkov, it was like she was being second-guessed sometimes. So she reshuffled her team, and she got him sent down. But I think the suspicion lingered that someone in the FBI was protecting the Merkovs."

"Did she venture who this person was?"

"She said she had concerns about a CIA guy on her team."

"Is that right? Does the name White ring a bell?"

"That's it. White. Curt White."

"I believe the FBI are now aware of him, sir, but that's only transpired in the last day or so."

"There's another."

"Another what?"

"Another name."

"On her team?"

"That's what she said to me, about two weeks ago. She had serious concerns over Curt White and Roy Stamper during both Merkov investigations."

Reznick took a few moments to let that bombshell sink in.

"Are you still there?"

"Yeah, sure, I'm still here. So that's a couple weeks ago she talked this over with you?"

"She knows she can trust me. She's my daughter."

"And she didn't tell anyone at the FBI. Even O'Donoghue?"

"That's right. She was paranoid that her concerns would get leaked. She said she had started compiling evidence."

"Evidence? Did she have any concrete evidence that they were conspiring against her?"

"She didn't have much, from what she said. She was building up a case in her spare time. But one thing she did have was a picture."

"A picture? What kind of picture?"

"A source of hers, a woman she'd trusted for many years—works at the Pentagon, former undergraduate at Duke. She passed her a picture of Curt White and Roy Stamper together."

"Is that so unusual?"

"The picture showed Curt White and Roy Stamper on their first day working for the CIA."

The information crashed through Reznick's head.

"How do you know?"

"Martha thought Stamper had started at the FBI straight out of Duke. It's not in his record that he worked at the CIA. But she looked into it. He spent two years at Langley in the Directorate of Analysis."

"And White?"

"Clandestine section. Martha said they both attended Duke with her source."

Reznick felt a jolt of anger deep inside him. He had trusted Stamper as implicitly as Meyerstein had over the years. He couldn't abide the thought of such deceit. He viewed Stamper as a traitor. A guy he had begun to have a grudging respect for in the hunt for Meyerstein. But it was all a front.

He wondered if Stamper had picked Curt White to be one of the CIA guys in the Hoover Building in DC. Maybe Stamper had been told by those within Langley that White was the operator who should be assigned.

The breach of trust hit Reznick hard in the guts. But, at the same time, he was also in awe of Meyerstein. She hadn't brushed aside her doubts over Stamper. Instead she had launched a secret investigation that had unearthed the CIA connection.

"Sir, one final thing," Reznick said, gathering his thoughts. "You say she was working on this in her spare time. I've heard that her electronic equipment was all taken away by the FBI."

"Martha always thought ahead. Like I taught her." Reznick was reminded in that instance of his late wife and the preparation she used to do for her job as a financial analyst.

"So, her notes she had typed up on the computer. Did she save the file to the cloud, or Dropbox?"

"No. She didn't want the information on any server, anywhere. So she saved it on a flash drive."

"A memory stick?"

"Yeah. But after she saved it, she always cleaned up her laptop so there were no traces of what she had written on the hard drive. Very meticulous about that."

"Sir, now this is very important—do you know where she put the flash drive?"

"Yes, I do."

"We're building up a picture of what has happened. This might be crucial. And it might lead us to her, we just don't know."

Meyerstein's father sighed. "This is killing me. Absolutely killing me. Her mother is beside herself with worry."

"Sir, where did she put the flash drive?"

"She made me promise not to tell anyone."

"Sir, I'm not anyone. You must trust me. Martha trusted me. And I want you to do the same. Can you do that?"

"There's a PVC pipe in her garage. Non-functioning. She places it in there, wrapped in waterproof plastic bag."

Reznick made a mental note.

"You find my girl, Jon. Bring her back to me. That's all I ask."

Reznick's mind was racing by the time he got back to the FBI's New York field office. He headed straight into O'Donoghue's office, where he relayed the new information.

The Director took a few moments to consider. "The best course of action in the circumstances is not to suspend. We need to let him carry on. Besides, we can't have him alerting anyone to what we know."

"I agree."

"But it would be beneficial if he was out of the way."

Reznick nodded.

"I'll tell him to head up to the penitentiary and interview the governor again."

"That'll do it. Thanks."

"It means we can press on with finding Martha Meyerstein." O'Donoghue bit his lower lip. "So, let's see . . . Bethesda. There's a new special agent, just been transferred in from Ohio to the Hoover Building. Never worked with or under Roy Stamper. I'll get her to retrieve the flash drive."

"Perfect."

O'Donoghue picked up the phone and called the agent directly. He stressed the confidential nature of his request and that the contents of the flash drive should be sent via encrypted email. He ended the call. "OK, that's done." Then he buzzed Roy Stamper into his office. "Need you up at the penitentiary. I'm thinking that the governor might be able to open this up, might have some intel from within the prison. Got to be worth another try, right?"

Stamper didn't look too sure but agreed. "I thought the focus was on New York City?"

"We've got that covered. I think this is an angle we need to look at again. I want you to try and turn the screw on this guy, Roy. Someone must know something about Dimitri Merkov up there that hasn't been passed on."

Stamper nodded. "Is Jon coming with me?"

"No, he's going to stay here. I want you to get on this, Roy. And you can interview the governor in the morning."

Stamper nodded. "Will do." He patted Reznick on his injured shoulder as he passed.

Reznick winced.

"Sorry, forgot. How you holding up, Jon?"

"Felt better, Roy. But we're going to find her."

When Stamper was out of the office, Reznick began to pace the room. "This whole thing. This CIA angle is not what I expected."

O'Donoghue nodded.

"So, what've we got? We've got that NYPD intelligence operative who is also working for the CIA, Schofield. Curt fucking White. Stamper. And the asset, Andrew Sparrow."

O'Donoghue shrugged. "What's your point?"

Reznick's mind began to race. "Hang on . . ."

"What?"

Reznick clicked his fingers. "Face recognition . . ."

"What about it?"

"Last I heard, the NYPD can tap into roughly six thousand street cameras, two-thirds of which are privately owned."

"Give or take, that's right."

"But I read there's also about seven thousand in public housing and across the city's subway stations."

"What's your point?"

"My point is, I'm assuming we're running face recognition as we speak, across the city."

"I should goddamn hope so. Which begs the question," O'Donoghue said, "why the hell haven't we picked up Schofield or White?"

"Great point," Reznick said.

O'Donoghue lifted his phone. "Have we or the NSA tried to do a trace on Schofield or Curt White in or around New York?" A long silence. "Then do it. Now!" He ended the call. "Son of a bitch!"

"What?"

"Special Agent Guillard, who works with Roy. He said Stamper had made clear he would take care of that."

"And had he?"

"Doesn't look like it. Guillard's saying Stamper must've forgotten or some bullshit."

Reznick felt himself grinding his teeth. "Fuck."

O'Donoghue rubbed his face. "Indeed."

The phone rang, and O'Donoghue picked up. He listened for a few moments. "I see. Interesting." Then he hung up.

"What?" Reznick asked.

"Guillard got the facial recognition guys to pull up anything in New York. Seems like they've already, this minute, got a hit. Schofield and White, with the asset in tow, not more than twenty blocks away."

"You can't be serious."

"I am."

"Where?"

O'Donoghue tapped a few keys on his laptop and turned it around. He showed Reznick a tracker showing their location. "This is them leaving a bank in Chinatown. We've got a positive fix on their car."

"I want in on this."

"You got it. You'll be with a plainclothes team, all Feds who work here in New York City. No links with Stamper. And you can call the shots. You'll have two handpicked Feds as your backup working from the Hoover Building. An NSA guy and cybersecurity expert. Any further questions?"

"Whatever it takes?"

O'Donoghue nodded. "Whatever it takes. You were brought in to help find Martha. So find her."

Fifty-Two

It was dark and Vladimir Merkov was standing on a deserted private beach, bathed in the light of a full moon, just beside his oceanfront East Hampton home. He inhaled his cigarette deeply and stared out at the water. He saw his breath in the chill of the evening. His audacious move had resulted in him getting his son out of jail, albeit at the expense of an FBI assistant director. But it had green-lit a strategic assassination, vital to securing his family's long-term business and financial future in America. He'd heard rumors for years that the CIA were interested in working with him. His closeness to his Moscow handlers had made that move impossible. Until now. But he knew changing sides was ultra-high risk.

The move to come within the CIA sphere of influence would threaten his vast web of legitimate businesses if he got caught in the crosshairs of the FBI. And the fact that every law enforcement agency in the world would have been alerted, including the Russian intelligence services, would put him on their radar. They would want to kill him or his son.

His closest confidants he had talked it over with had said to his face that this wasn't a smart move.

Merkov hadn't made a rash move in his life since he'd left for America. He'd retreated into the shadows, any trace of his old life obliterated. New companies sprung up, old ones wound up, and safe-deposit boxes were opened and stuffed with diamonds and fine jewels, paintings by Van Gogh and Monet. And all the time he'd increased his wealth and became a billionaire. He dealt exclusively in two commodities: gold and cash. To be precise, the dollar. Suitcases of dollars. Deposit boxes with backpacks of cocaine were exchanged for dollars. He hooked up with the Colombians, and his associates spread the cocaine across North America. The money was an avalanche.

It meant he could move around. Ten thousand dollars got you a great fake passport. He had dozens.

Thanks to his health, his days were numbered. But he had been reassured by the CIA that they would offer greater long-term protection than the Russians for his family—including his son and estranged wife—not to mention his business interests, once he was in the ground.

Out of his peripheral vision, some movement.

Merkov turned and saw Don Lagunov crossing the dunes toward him. He was a Russian émigré and financier, as well as a close adviser. They began to walk along the beach together.

Merkov dragged hard on his cigarette. "What's the latest news?"

"Dimitri made the meet. And the money has gone through, as Mr. Dragović requested."

Merkov nodded. His son's details had had to be sent to Dragović to confirm the request was legitimate. His son was the only person authorized to do the financial transfer. "Has Dragović confirmed he is in place?"

"He's set."

"Good. So where is Dimitri?"

"He's safe. And well. You know how he is."

Merkov smiled and closed his eyes. His crazy son was still his flesh and blood. "When will I see him?"

"A matter of hours. Tell me, when is Meyerstein going to be released? I need to get my guys an hour's notice so they can get out of there."

Merkov sighed. "I'll decide."

"Look, you don't need to keep her anymore. Besides, she's in a bad way."

"She's to be kept with us until the operation is complete."

Lagunov shook his head. "We double-crossed them. They're not going to like that. And she's gonna die on us."

"This is how I want to do it."

"Vladimir, you're making this personal. This seems to me to be about you allowing this Meyerstein to get into your head. I know you swore to avenge your son's incarceration. I understand that. It's natural. Up to a point. But you need to let it go. You need to let her go. You got Dimitri out and he has green-lit this operation you wanted, right?"

Merkov inhaled on the cigarette one last time, sucking the smoke down deep into his lungs, before he flicked it into the dark water. "Don't ever tell me how to run my business. I gave my word. And my word I will keep."

"Vladimir, how long have we known each other?"

"Too long."

"Sooner or later they will find her. The switch was foolish."

Merkov sighed. He was no longer in the mood to listen to the advice of others. He had so little time.

Lagunov leaned in close. "Make no mistake, when the FBI get to you, every one of us will be brought down. Every Russian in America will be implicated in some way. They will not stop until every one of us is destroyed."

"Once Dragović has carried out the operation, Meyerstein will be freed," replied Merkov. "I give you my word."

Fifty-Three

Reznick winced as he felt his shoulder burning. He was sat in the passenger seat of a Lincoln headed north on I-95. Curt White had been replaced by a tough-looking Fed named Frankie, who was using an iPad to monitor the GPS position of the vehicle Schofield was traveling in.

"They're about one point three miles ahead of us."

Reznick saw a sign up ahead for New Rochelle. "So, what do you think? We intercept, or we watch and wait?"

Frankie blew out his cheeks. "My problem with watch and wait is we might lose them. It sounds crazy, but it happens. Technology isn't failsafe. But they might just head back into town and await instructions. Or they might not have information on the whereabouts of the assistant director."

"You know what I think? We intercept. We go in hard. And fast—when they don't expect it."

"Jon, I copy what you're saying. I say let's do this."

"How about we wait until we get an empty stretch of road, and then do it."

"Fine by me."

An hour later they were still headed north and into Connecticut. Reznick looked at the driver. "Let's get this underway."

"You want to do this now?"

Reznick turned around to Frankie. "How far behind are we?"

"Five hundred yards, maybe less."

"We're the lead car on this." Reznick flicked open his radio. "Do we copy on that?"

"Affirmative," said the voice in the second car that they had just overtaken.

Reznick put down the radio and pulled out the 9mm Beretta from his waistband. He pulled back the slide. "Frankie, you good?"

Frankie put down the iPad and pulled out his Glock. "I'm always ready."

Reznick spotted the SUV a couple of hundred yards ahead on the freeway. "Hardly any traffic," he said, "which is very good." He turned to the driver again. "Gradual acceleration."

The driver hit the gas as they closed in on the SUV.

Fifty-Four

Brent Schofield was sitting in the back seat with Sparrow, headed for the safe house, when his cell phone rang.

"Are you OK to talk?"

"Go right ahead, sir."

"I just got a message confirming that Dragović is en route. And we're underway finally. Money transferred. Very well played, Brent."

"Thank you, sir."

"I've bought us some time with regards to your boss at the NYPD," Charles said. "I've drafted in a replacement so you can complete this operation."

"Much appreciated, sir."

"Now, with regards to the asset . . . can you put him on speaker?"

Schofield pressed a button on his phone and turned to Sparrow. "My boss wants a word."

"Yeah . . . ?" Sparrow said.

"I hope you're feeling slightly better after your ordeal."

"Yes I am, thank you."

"My colleagues are taking you to a suburban safe house, and we already have your new American citizenship papers, signed and sealed. And the matching identity. The works. I trust this is in order."

"Thank you."

Schofield turned off the speaker and pressed the phone to his ear. "Sir, anything else? The address?"

There was a pause. "We'll send that in ten minutes."

Curt White glanced in his side mirror. "Goddamn!"

"What is it?" Schofield asked.

"Tailgating fucker right up my tailpipe!"

Suddenly, the SUV was hit from behind and started chaotically spinning out of control. The traffic on the freeway was going crazy in all directions. Schofield turned around. In that split second he saw, farther back down the road, Reznick in the passenger seat of the car that had hit them.

The SUV flipped over and Schofield smashed his head against the shattered glass. Shards of glass embedded in his skin. The pain burned and he groaned. Time seemed to stand still. He tasted blood. Heard the sound of moaning from those around him. The sound of crunching metal and brakes, as the smell of burning rubber, smoke, and gasoline filled the car.

"Brent, what's happening? Talk to me!"

Fifty-Five

The SUV was billowing smoke and emitting a piercing alarm as Reznick hauled Schofield out of a smashed window. Blood spilled from a head wound.

Reznick pressed a gun to the man's forehead. "On the ground now, fucker."

Schofield fell to his knees. He was handcuffed by a Fed, his arms in front, and slumped on the grass verge. He was frisked, a cell phone found in his jacket pocket and a Glock in a shoulder holster. Both were handed over to Reznick.

Frankie bundled Andrew Sparrow to the ground and quickly handcuffed him. A cell phone and two keys were retrieved from his jacket. "Mr. Lermontov, I presume."

Sparrow refused to acknowledge him.

Reznick headed around to the driver's side and pulled Curt White out of the vehicle, semiconscious, blood spilling from his ears. He handcuffed him too. "You double-crossing fuck!" he shouted.

"Nothing personal, Reznick. Just business."

Reznick grabbed his head and smashed it through the glass. "Likewise."

Blood poured from Curt's face. His eyes rolled back in his head. Then he blacked out.

A Fed hauled the motionless CIA man into the back of the second FBI car.

Cars whizzed by. Reznick turned around and stared at Schofield. "Well, this is nice and cozy, huh?" He pulled out Schofield's cell phone and scrolled through the incoming-call numbers. He spoke into his lapel mic. "Grady, are you hearing me?"

The NSA guy attached to Reznick's team, working out of DC, spoke: "Go ahead, Jon."

"I've got Schofield's cell." He gave the number of the phone. "Is it bringing up anything?"

"Gimme a sec." Reznick heard the tapping of a keyboard. "Registered to Max Charles, Fairfax, Virginia."

"Tell me the name of the last person who called Schofield."

A beat. "Interesting. Same name. Seems like a lot of calls from Max Charles."

"Get a GPS fix on Charles's current location, if that's possible. And get me everything we have on Charles. Also a geotag on the locations Schofield has been."

"Hold the line, Jon."

Reznick paced beside the crashed SUV, smoke still billowing from the engine. "ASAP, my friend."

"The main stop was the Industrial and Commercial Bank of China, downtown Manhattan."

"Get this information to Director O'Donoghue. And only him. There are two keys, too, so it might be a safe-deposit box."

Eventually, Grady came back on the line. "Jon, I've now pulled up footage from inside the bank, with Schofield, Sparrow, and a few others in the vault."

"Bingo. Tell O'Donoghue to get a team in there quick. No questions."

"Hang on . . ."

"What is it?"

"Face recognition is pinging my attention to one of the faces who's with them."

Reznick closed his eyes. It seemed to take a lifetime for him to receive the name.

"Fuck a duck. Dimitri Merkov, no less, with two members of the Russian mafia in tow."

His mind was racing. "Tell Director O'Donoghue everything. And tell him direct. Got it?"

"Leave it with me."

Reznick hustled a handcuffed Andrew Sparrow into the back of the nearest vehicle. "Soon as you have something, no matter how seemingly insignificant," he said to Grady, "I want to know."

The line went dead.

Fifty-Six

Andrej Dragović was driving past the MetLife Stadium in East Rutherford, New Jersey—home of the Giants and the Jets—when his cell phone rang.

"How's the Dragon today?"

Dragović grinned. "Finally, I get to talk to the man."

"Hey, I've been busy. Listen, the money has all gone through to your account, and the rest is pending upon delivery. So that means you can see it, but you can't touch until the operation is completed."

"I was wondering why I hadn't heard from you in person."

"I've been out of circulation, as you might have heard."

"I heard all right. Just thought you'd be able to make calls."

"Not worth the risk, we thought."

"Smart."

"But I'm back. And I'm as bad as ever."

Dragović laughed. "You crazy fucker."

"You better believe it, my friend. OK, so here's what's going to happen. You drop the car off on any quiet, residential street in Moonachie. You far?"

"The satnav has it at only two miles away. So I'm on the outskirts."

"Tiny little place. But ideal. You drop it off wherever you like. And you get a Line 161 bus to Manhattan. Port Authority Bus Terminal."

"Got it, 161. Then what?"

"You make your way to the Howard Johnson in Chinatown. Get a good night's sleep. In your room will be a smart polo shirt, nice jeans, and sneakers—the usual attire for the delivery guy apparently."

"Then what?"

"Tomorrow morning, bright and early, you head to a parking garage in East Village. Quik Park, East 14th Street. The vehicle you requested will be waiting."

Fifty-Seven

Reznick grabbed Sparrow by the throat and stared into his eyes. He exerted pressure on the carotid artery. "Here's what's going to happen, Sparrow, or whatever you like to call yourself. I'm going to get an answer this time. If not, I will dispose of you myself."

Sparrow's eyes filled with tears as Reznick exerted more pressure with his thumbs.

"I told the truth!"

"You lying sack of shit."

"I swear!"

"You lied to me. And you know what I said I would do?"

"Please, I deal with investment strategies, I don't know what you're talking about."

"You got a lucky break before. You've had your nine lives. Now you're going to tell me the truth. And, believe me, you *will* tell me the truth."

"What do you want to know?"

"I asked you where the assistant director was. You mentioned Hart Island. Well, we checked. She wasn't there."

"I swear to God, that's where she was."

Reznick pressed his thumbs tighter into the man's neck. "Now listen, you stupid fuck, do not mess with me. I will kill you if you lie to me again."

"I'm telling you the truth! She's there!"

"We checked! That's bullshit."

"How many times do I have to tell you, she was there!"

"Shut the fuck up!"

"I'm not lying! She was there! I heard her!"

Reznick released his neck for a moment. "You heard her?"

"Yes, I was there."

"When? Tell me!"

"Forty-eight hours ago."

Reznick called Grady.

"Still working on it, Jon?"

"Grady, check Sparrow's GPS to see if he was at any location on Hart Island that was previously searched."

"Now?"

"Right fucking now."

A pause. "Jon, we're running that as we speak. We've got a track on where he was."

"Was he on Hart Island?"

A silence opened up down the line. "No."

"You lying piece of—"

"However . . . Wait, Jon, at 02:43 hours we have him at North Brother Island, two nights ago."

"Say again, where was he?"

"North Brother Island. It's deserted. Site of an abandoned old hospital. Slap bang in the middle of the East River."

Reznick released Sparrow and got out of earshot of those in the car.

"East River? Fuck! Listen to me, Grady, pass this to the Director. Message him. Do you understand? North Brother Island. Top priority. I repeat, this is top, top priority. But it's also classified. Top secret. So not a word to anyone apart from O'Donoghue."

"Copy that, Jon."

"Strictly need-to-know. Get back to me if you get anything else. This is critical."

Reznick ended the call. He looked into the car, where Sparrow was holding his neck, tears streaming down his face. "My colleague says you were not telling the truth. Do you want to explain why you were visiting an abandoned hospital on an uninhabited island on the East River?"

Sparrow closed his eyes. "What? That's not correct. They took me, blindfolded, and told me I was going to Hart Island in Long Island Sound."

Reznick took a few moments to let his words sink in. "Blindfolded?"

"I swear, I'm telling you what they told me."

Reznick could see what had happened. "They told you you were going to Hart Island . . . Don't you get it? Fuck! They hoodwinked you. Big time."

Sparrow shook his head. "They're scary people. You do as you're told. Look after his money. His companies. I know the keys to everything he has. His son is a scary guy, believe me."

"How did you get there? Tell me about that."

"I got a call. I was picked up at some place on the Bronx waterfront, and taken on a boat, blindfolded. It was pretty intense."

"Why did you have to see him in person?"

"Mr. Merkov needed to sign some documents."

"Did you ask why you were having to do it there?"

"Yes, I did."

"And what did he say?"

"Told me to mind my own business. He signed, then I was blindfolded again, and the boat took me back."

"What's the place like?"

"The place I was taken was a sprawling, creepy place. All abandoned, overgrown . . . old buildings, staircases, plant and coal houses, smokestack too. I was under the assumption it was Hart Island."

"What else do I need to know?"

"I can't say too much more . . ."

"You need to be honest with me if you're not going to be packed off on a rendition flight direct to Moscow, my friend. Trust me, Merkov is not going to save you now. No one can. Except you. So spill the fucking beans."

"I'm working for the CIA."

"Might've fucking guessed. What did you do for Merkov?"

"In a nutshell, we were both working for the CIA. I disappeared money offshore, via a law firm in Delaware set up by Langley."

"So the Agency knew what Merkov was up to all along?"

"Some people did."

"I'd imagine you must have some contact with Mr. Merkov on the phone?"

"Never. I'm contacted by iMessage and then directed."

"Who messages you?"

"I have no idea."

Reznick weighed up the information. He could see where the misdirection by Merkov and his men would have helped their aim of concealing Meyerstein's location.

He called Grady and asked for any updates.

"Was just about to call you, Jon. Huge money transfer. From a company which we believe might be controlled by friends of Dimitri Merkov to an unknown account in Switzerland."

"Get to the bottom of that. And keep the Director, and only him, in the loop."

"OK."

"Anything else?"

"He sent a message," Grady said.

"Who sent a message?"

"Dimitri Merkov."

"When?"

"When the ten million dollars was transferred, he sent a message which we've already decrypted."

"What did it say?"

"*My father sends his love and respect. And a further ten million dollars will be transferred to your Zurich account on delivery.*"

"What do they mean, *delivery*?" asked Reznick.

"Could mean anything. Weapons? Money? Is that what this is about—just money? But for what purpose? Drugs?"

"Explain."

"Merkov and his associates are involved in the trafficking of heroin, ecstasy, amphetamines, and just about every substance under the sun," Grady said.

"Vladimir Merkov wouldn't need his son on the outside to do that," Reznick said. "Still doesn't add up."

"Drugs trafficking gives them unbelievable financial power and muscle."

Reznick wondered what exactly the real purpose of the huge money transfer was, and how it connected to the release of Dimitri Merkov. It couldn't just be drugs.

He thought of Vladimir Merkov. And he thought of Merkov's son. "They kill for fun, right?"

"Oh yeah. That's how they control the hundreds of enforcers and their gangs. People step out of line, they die."

"But I'd imagine Vladimir would be able to order hits through a chain of command." Reznick contemplated the Merkov empire, built on violence and sustained by money. "What if they were paying for a hit. But not an ordinary hit. A high-profile assassination."

Grady was silent.

"Update the Director with that information. Do you hear me? Give him the bullet points of what we've learned. Got to go."

A few minutes after ending the call, Reznick's cell phone rang.

"Jon, it's Director O'Donoghue."

"Sir."

"I have a team of analysts working on this information as we speak."

"Excellent. Can I give you some advice, sir?"

"Shoot."

"There have been complications. We've got a situation developing with the release of money by Dimitri Merkov."

"We've already got a team working on hunting him down."

"My main concern is Martha."

"Mine too. So you believe North Brother Island is where she's being kept?"

"Very possibly. But here's the problem. The easiest thing in the world would be to go in with a twenty-man team and hunt her down. Choppers. Maybe a SWAT team or SEALs. But there are red flags all over this. We don't have time to do field reconnaissance. Another complication is there are numerous buildings on the island. I'm also not convinced that Vladimir Merkov will still be on the island. And, leaving that aside, the men he'll have looking after her will be on strict orders to kill her if there's any rescue attempt."

"That's a pretty fair assessment."

"Sir, our top priority is clearly to get Martha back. But we need to know she's still alive."

"What if we sent up a drone that was able to monitor cell phone conversations on the island?" O'Donoghue said.

"Phenomenal."

"Leave that with me."

"This could be the endgame. I can't see how they're going to release her. I think they planned to kill her all along, if they haven't already. With Dimitri Merkov released and the money transferred, not to mention the activation of this delivery, I can only see one outcome."

"Would it be worthwhile trying to make contact with Merkov or his associates again at this late hour?"

"They've pissed all over us. He might just want to tease us and do it all over again . . ."

O'Donoghue sighed. "That he has."

"Sir, I know the FBI are well equipped to deal with this, but after everything that's happened, I'd like to do this."

"Are you serious?"

"Deadly. What do we know about this island?"

"Pretty sketchy. Old abandoned hospital."

"Electricity?"

"Probably not," O'Donoghue said. "But I'm guessing they're not sitting around in candlelight. So I'd say there's maybe a generator on site."

Reznick's mind ran ahead as he began to formulate a plan. It would need the cover of darkness. Night-vision goggles.

"Let's get the drone up first and get a preliminary assessment," said the Director.

"You better get a move on. We need to go tonight."

Fifty-Eight

Martha Meyerstein tasted blood when she came to. She squinted as the tears spilled down her face. Terrible pain tore through her knee. She could just about make out some silhouetted figures at the far end of the room. Exposed wrought-iron pipes. Where the hell was she?

"You're back with us," said someone with a Russian accent. The smell of cigarette smoke.

Meyerstein was breathing hard.

"How are you today?"

Meyerstein closed her eyes. Images of her children flashed up in her mind. She imagined them sitting in a safe house, wondering where she was. Cindy would be doing her best to reassure Jacob. Her son might even have regressed to wetting the bed. She knew he was an anxious child. He needed her there. She knew the FBI would be doing everything in their power to get her released. But she also knew that the people she was dealing with were callous, murderous thugs, and wouldn't think twice about torturing and killing her. The way they'd laughed in her face after kneecapping her lingered in her mind. Their leering, stupid faces. The smell of liquor on their breath. She knew the gunshot wound would be infected. Too much time had passed.

She began to shiver. She felt a draft on her face. She sensed she was slowly dying. Hour by hour. Minute by minute. She was bleeding out. The wound would be septic.

The more she thought of her kidnapping from a Bethesda road, the more she realized this wasn't chance. They'd got help on the inside. Someone within the FBI. Perhaps someone on her team. She thought of the first day she'd joined the FBI with Roy Stamper, little knowing that he had already been a CIA operative for more than two years. Was this really the result of his actions? She felt sick at the betrayal. Were there others? She thought back to the original investigation into Vladimir Merkov. Notes going missing. Files incomplete.

Her mistake had been not to take the concerns she had—especially the photographic proof of Stamper and White at Langley—direct to O'Donoghue. But her thinking at the time had become clouded. She'd thought the Director was more likely to take Stamper's side. Now, unbelievably, *no one* would know.

She heard disembodied voices in the cold November breeze. Russian voices. She knew they were talking about her.

"Hey!" one of them said, snapping her out of her semiconscious state.

Meyerstein struggled to open her eyes. She saw blurred faces in the harsh light. Then a cell phone was pressed to her face.

"What's your name?"

"My name is Martha Meyerstein, Assistant Director of the FBI. 10-45C. I repeat, 10-45C."

The cell phone was taken from her.

More whispered conversations.

Then it all went black.

Fifty-Nine

Bill O'Donoghue stared at the large split screen on the wall of the conference room as he held an emergency briefing with Homeland Security and the CIA. On another screen was the still image of Martha Meyerstein. A third screen was showing night-vision drone footage of North Brother Island on the East River.

"So, Bill, this is looking pretty bleak," the Secretary of Homeland Security said. "The footage shows her in a terrible condition. She's been shot. Blood loss. Major trauma. And no medical treatment. The police code she gave, 10-45C, is telling us her medical condition is critical."

"Tell me about the drone."

"The first thing I would say is there is good news. North Brother Island is where she is being held, of that we're sure."

"We're positive on that?"

"We're monitoring cell phone conversations from those on the island. Three have already been picked up in the last hour, with GPS pinpointing North Brother Island as the location where the footage was sent from."

"And this island has been deserted for decades?"

"It was. Not anymore. GPS analysis from the phones we've locked onto across the island shows she is there right now. The microphones on the cell phones have been remotely activated by the FBI and we've verified her voice. And we believe there might be four other people on the island."

"So assuming we decide to go in . . . ?"

CIA Director Henry Cain signaled for a chance to speak. "Bill, from the outset, I just want to say the Central Intelligence Agency are conducting a high-level investigation into the events. I'm told that this was not authorized at any level within the CIA. Max Charles is retired. But I also want to believe there are a lot of lessons to be learned as regards information-sharing. I think we can all agree there has been some unfortunate overlap and misunderstandings in what has happened."

O'Donoghue shifted in his seat. "There have been no misunderstandings on our side, Henry. And you know goddamn well you were playing your fucking games."

Cain shook his head. "I don't accept that, Bill."

"Your guys were protecting a CIA asset, who is effectively Merkov's private banker. And at the expense of an FBI assistant director? Quite despicable." He didn't mention anything about the suspicions Meyerstein had about Roy Stamper and Curt White. That was for further down the line.

"I don't think that's a fair assessment. I think there's been a blurring of boundaries and objectives, no question. But I understand how you must feel."

"Do you?"

"Listen, we all know, shit happens."

"Are you saying this was a rogue operation?"

"We don't know for sure. We're working under that assumption. Max Charles, I'm led to believe, is a non-executive director of a North Carolina-based geopolitical security consultancy, Global Reach Solutions, with several former CIA operatives."

"Sounds plausible. But I don't buy it. I believe this was made to look like a rogue operation if the shit hit the fan."

Cain said nothing.

"But that's for the birds. At this moment I don't give a damn about this asset Andrew Sparrow, or whatever the hell his name is."

"I must interject here, Bill," Cain said. "This is all about an American asset who has penetrated a web of companies that Russians and the Russian government have used for well over a decade. So before we get all high and mighty and go all gung-ho on this, we need to slow the hell down."

O'Donoghue said, "Just so everyone knows, a CIA operator shot a man who was helping the FBI with this investigation."

"Come, come, Director, why so coy?" Cain said. "The man in question was none other than Jon Reznick, was it not? Ex-Delta Force, trained assassin. Weren't you the one who criticized his presence on Meyerstein's task force a couple years back?"

"Reznick was shot by one of your guys. You need to rein these fuckers in."

"Our guy was, I'm told, protecting a vital asset with national security intel."

The Secretary of Homeland Security put up his hand as if calling for quiet. "This will get us nowhere. We shouldn't conflate different issues. Bill, where is Andrew Sparrow at this moment?"

"With the FBI."

"I'm happy with that at present. But at some time in the near future, we need the asset back under the auspices of the CIA."

"That can be arranged, once Martha is back safe and sound."

The Secretary of Homeland Security leaned back in his seat. "Bill, this isn't up for discussion."

"You're damn right it's not. Here's how it's going to work. We get Martha Meyerstein back, with each and every agency focused on that task, pooling and sharing everything we have."

"Bill, this can't be conditional."

"Listen, first we get Martha back. And once she's been retrieved, hopefully still alive, you get the asset. Also, it's worth mentioning here that there is also a live operation afoot. Did you know about that, Henry? Did the CIA know about that?"

Cain stared out from the screen. "What are you talking about?"

"The FBI has evidence that an assassin, a Serb, financed by the Russian mob—perhaps with the full knowledge of elements within the CIA—has been hired for an assassination. Andrej Dragović is his name. Has links with the Merkovs, going back years."

Cain was quiet.

"I have a team focused on finding Dragović. I'll keep you updated throughout the day. But as it stands, my number-one goal is getting Martha Meyerstein back. Once this is all over, and you want to discuss national interests, offshore companies, and Russian influence in America—fine, but as of now, there must unanimous focus on bringing Martha Meyerstein back home."

Nods on the screen.

"And what about the whereabouts of Vladimir Merkov?" O'Donoghue said. "The analysis we have is that he is not on the island. It's just his thugs, along with Meyerstein. So where the hell is he? Also, Henry, you wanna enlighten us as to how the Russian consulate are dealing with one of their guys being iced? Military attaché Sokolov. Murdered. Was this at the behest of Merkov senior?"

Cain shifted in his seat. "Things are somewhat fraught, as you can imagine."

"First things first. We get Martha Meyerstein back. Now, if that's all, gentlemen, I've got work to do."

Sixty

As the night wore on, the aerial drone's reconnaissance photos of North Brother Island were pinned to a wall in the Director's office in Lower Manhattan.

"Jon, to attempt an operation to rescue her, without any planning, is madness. That's what everyone says. They say, sure they could get in—take one, maybe two, perhaps even three down—but the risk to Martha would be too high."

"That's bullshit, sir, with respect. Of course there are risks. If we become so risk-averse, we'll do nothing."

"Jon, my best analysts said it would be a kamikaze mission, without any guarantee of success."

"I'm telling you that is incorrect analysis. We need to act. And we need to do it right fucking now."

"Jon, we got this. But it'll take time."

"We haven't got time. We need to go in."

"My gut is telling me the same thing, Jon. But my head says otherwise. We need to do this right. This is on a whole new level. The problem? There'd be ninety percent chance of Martha getting killed if this was undertaken. They've suggested a Navy SEAL team for this. But it'll take twelve hours to get them in place."

"We're clean out of time. I'll do this myself."

"Whoa . . . Hang on, Jon. What are you saying?"

"I'm saying I'll do this. Just me. And with backup on shore."

"That's not going to happen. That's insane."

"Sir, I got this. Trust me."

O'Donoghue turned and stared at the night-vision photos of the island taken from the drone.

"She's there, sir. She's there now."

The Director sighed. "I'm well aware of that."

"Sir, look at me."

O'Donoghue turned around and looked at Reznick.

"What do you see?"

"I don't understand."

"I asked, what do you see?"

"I see a guy. Special ops. I think you're borderline crazy."

"Maybe I am. But I will find her. I swear to God, I'll bring her back. SWAT teams, SEAL teams, they take time to arrive, prepare . . . You're right on that point. Sometimes too many moving parts. But I'm here. And I will fucking guarantee I am the best opportunity for getting her back safe and sound. Twelve hours' time, she'll be dead."

O'Donoghue ran his hand through his hair. "I need to think this over."

"Did this breakthrough come through diligence and FBI procedures, sir?"

"No, it did not."

"We've fought and scraped to get this far. And we haven't played by the rules and regulations bullshit. We're still in the game. But for how much longer?"

The Director sighed. "What do you need?"

"I need you to get me into position."

"What else?"

"I need backup on shore. I need night-vision goggles. And I need a 9mm Berretta with silencer, a rifle with night-vision sights, and a good knife. Also a first-aid kit with morphine and bandages."

"How are you going to do this?"

Reznick's mind was racing ahead. His years in Delta had prepared him for the most dangerous missions, including high-risk hostage rescue. He thought of Meyerstein, cowering and alone on the island. But he was already beginning to formulate a plan to get her back. "Leave that to me."

Sixty-One

Just after midnight, and after being provided with pain relief and Dexedrine by an FBI doctor, Reznick pushed off from the Bronx shoreline in the kayak. In the distance he could see the lights of Rikers Island. He paddled toward his first stop, South Brother Island, in the inky darkness. He had a backpack with all the essentials he would need. His heart was racing with the exertion but also an adrenaline rush, knowing what lay ahead. Slowly, his eyes were becoming accustomed to the darkness.

After a few hundred yards, his earpiece crackled into life.

"Jon, you're doing good," said the voice of a Fed back on the shore. "You should be around one hundred and twenty yards from the beach of South Brother Island. I repeat, one hundred and twenty yards. Do you copy?"

Reznick could just make out sand in the distance. "Yeah, copy that, got it."

He paddled hard through the choppy waters. Then he jumped out in the shallows and pulled the kayak up onto the beach.

Reznick took out the night-vision binoculars from his backpack. He saw a light in the algae-green tinge—just over three hundred yards away—on the supposedly deserted neighboring North Brother Island. Maybe a phone light, he couldn't be sure.

He turned around and saw the oil terminal at Port Morris in the distance.

"Jon, do you hear me?" O'Donoghue's voice in his earpiece.

"Sir, hearing you loud and clear." He looked up and saw the drone, high up in the sky. "Any updates?"

"We are one hundred percent confident there are four people on the island, in addition to Martha. Her voice is faint but discernible in the background."

Reznick knew the Feds had turned one of Merkov's guys' cell phones into a roving bug, activating the microphone to hear what was being said. "Where exactly are they?"

"There's an overgrown road going north–south. On one side is an abandoned maintenance building. But across from that is what I'm told is the hospital's old nurses' residence. The generator has been hooked up in there."

"What else? More details."

"Four men, all Russian. One speaks very good English. He's Merkov's main man. Voice analysis is showing him as Martin Zhukov, infamous Moscow-born thug and enforcer. With him are three guys from his crew. From Staten Island. One of the three is periodically scanning the perimeter of the island. Like a lookout."

"Which side of the island?"

"Opposite side from you."

"Which would leave Zhukov and two of his guys somewhere in this nurses' residence."

"It's exposed to the elements. We're also picking up that they're getting loaded."

"On what?"

"What do you think? Vodka. Cocaine."

"Sounds like a party."

"So . . . pretty unpredictable elements at work."

Reznick sighed.

"You OK?"

The sound of police sirens drifting across the stretch of water from the Bronx reminded Reznick how close they were to the shore. He looked over toward North Brother Island. No sign of movement.

"I'm good. I've got this."

"Best of luck, Jon. We're all rooting for you."

Reznick put the night-vision binoculars in his backpack, which he placed back in the kayak. Then he dragged the kayak back into the water and pushed off. He began paddling across the East River to the overgrown, long-forgotten island.

Sixty-Two

Reznick pulled the kayak high onto the beach of North Brother Island, adjacent to the jetty. He picked up the backpack with his gear in it, hauled it across the sand, and hunkered down behind a stone wall. He unzipped his bag and pulled out his night-vision binoculars. He could hear voices, and even music. Through the foliage he saw buildings. Then he saw a figure nodding his head to the beat, smoking a cigarette and checking his cell phone.

Reznick reckoned the guy was about sixty yards away. He could head toward him. But the amount of broken trees, branches, and crumbling brickwork meant that he risked alerting the man to his presence.

He reached into his backpack and pulled out the rifle and the silencer. He clicked them into place, took aim, and flicked off the safety.

Reznick had the man in the crosshairs of the night-vision sight. He held his breath as the man kept on moving his head. He pulled the trigger. A muffled *phut*. The man collapsed into the undergrowth, music still playing on his cell phone. Birds scattered into the dark sky.

He put on the backpack, rifle still aimed at the lifeless body as he moved forward through the undergrowth. Senses switched on. The night vision was picking out birds in the trees, and the residual warmth from the corpse of the man he'd just killed. He bent down and picked up the dead guy's cell phone, putting it in his jacket pocket.

Not far away, the sound of a man's voice, barking instructions in Russian.

Reznick crouched down, only yards from the body of the lookout. He watched and waited. Heart pounding. He sensed the man's presence.

"Sacha!" a man's voice shouted. "Sacha!"

Slowly, into view from Reznick's right, came a bear of a man holding a radio. It crackled into life. Indecipherable Russian voices.

"Sacha!" the man shouted, making his way to the beach.

The man stopped still, maybe six or seven yards away. He turned around and peered into the undergrowth, then trudged toward the body.

Reznick realized that shooting the man with the radio might alert his colleagues, who could be listening in. He took off his backpack and took the knife from the sheath on his belt. He crept up behind the man and hooked his right arm around the man's neck. Then he plunged the knife deep into his throat. The man gargled for a second, then slumped to the ground.

Reznick pulled the knife out, wiped it clean, and re-sheathed it on his belt. He picked up the man's radio, then rifled through the dead man's pockets and pulled out a cell phone, which he put in his back pocket. Then he found a Glock in a shoulder holster. He moved over to where he'd left his backpack and put the Glock inside. He had taken two out of the game. Only two remained.

The radio crackled into life. "Vadim!"

Reznick didn't answer.

"Vadim!"

Reznick switched the radio off and dropped it in the overgrown grass. Further down he spotted a faint glow of light. It was coming from the dilapidated nursing quarters.

He knew the easiest thing to do would be to head straight there. Instead, he double-backed. A bird flew out of a tree and brushed his face. He grimaced, teeth clenched. He began to run through some scenarios in his head. He could see how it was going to pan out.

He circumnavigated the ruined shell of the nurses' quarters. The glow of the light became brighter.

Reznick saw he was nearing what appeared to be the rear of the building. There was a space where a door had been. Particles of dust drifting in the eerie darkness caught in his throat. He pressed his ear against the stone wall. The muffled sound of whispers.

He held his breath and craned his neck around the opening. Wooden stairs. The light was coming from upstairs.

Suddenly, raised voices.

"Fuck you!"

Then a creaking as someone descended the wooden stairs. Reznick pulled back and crouched out of sight. He knew what he was going to do. He waited until the man exited the building and went in the direction of the beach, a gun in one hand, a radio in the other.

Reznick headed in. And up the stairs, two at a time.

A voice from upstairs shouted, "Sacha, is that you, you lazy son of a bitch?"

Reznick got to the second-floor landing. The light was coming from a room farther down the hall.

"Sacha!"

"*Da?*" Reznick said. The butt of the scoped rifle was firmly pressed against the pocket of his right shoulder. He took a step forward and saw a man sitting in a chair. Reznick shot him twice in the head. He let off a third shot. But it jammed.

Fuck.

He headed into an adjoining room. Empty.

Fuck. Where the hell is she?

He put down the rifle and pulled on the night-vision goggles. He spread-eagled himself on the floor and took the Beretta from his waistband.

A few seconds later, he heard footsteps running up the stairs.

Reznick saw the man's terrified look. He aimed for the thigh. Then he squeezed the trigger. The man screamed, clutching his leg, and collapsed on the ground.

Reznick didn't move. He saw the man was still clutching a gun. So Reznick shot his hand, taking off two fingers, finally releasing the man's grip. The screaming became an anguished moan.

He scrambled over to the man, kicked the gun away, and pressed the Beretta to his forehead. "Where is she? Answer and you live."

The man had tears in his eyes. He stared, as if unbelieving.

Reznick pressed the gun tighter to the man's temple. "I'll count to three. And then you'll die."

He began the count.

"One . . . two . . . thr—"

"Stop! Cellar. Basement."

"Where's the entrance?"

"Under the stairs, there's a door. Steps lead down into the basement."

"Why should I believe you?"

"Please . . . I beg you." The man was shaking, in deep shock. Bleeding out. "Please, get me help?"

Reznick went through the man's pockets, pulled out a gun, and kicked it across the room. He knew that the Feds could interview him later and find out exactly what he knew. He was part of the Merkov crew. And that could be invaluable.

Reznick took off the man's belt and hauled him over to an old radiator. Then he tied him tight to it. The man was unable to move, blood spilling from his hand. But to make sure, he ripped off the Russian's shirt and tied his arms to the radiator, too. "Are you lying?"

"I swear . . . please get me help."

Reznick turned away as the man began to scream once more. The night-vision goggles highlighted more dust particles as he headed down the old stairs. He saw the small door and opened it, climbing down into the pitch-black cellar. In the corner, tied to a chair, was Martha Meyerstein.

Her head was slumped forward, blood congealing at her ankles, knee shot to pieces.

Reznick took off his goggles and backpack. He pulled out the medical kit. He first cleaned up her wound, and popped two soluble morphine tablets in her mouth. He untied her from the chair. Then he slung her over his shoulder.

He picked up the backpack and slung it over his other shoulder. She whispered, "Jon?" as he climbed back up the stairs and headed out of the doorway. The man's screaming from upstairs was echoing around the old brick walls.

Reznick carried Meyerstein through the undergrowth, skirting the bodies of the men he'd killed.

Then back down to the beach.

Reznick laid her on the sand. He felt her pulse. Very faint. He put down the backpack and took out a flare. Then he fired it high into the sky above the East River. He heard a frantic voice in his earpiece.

"Reznick! Reznick! Gimme the code!"

"It's code 4231. I repeat, code 4231. Chopper. Paramedics needed."

"Hang in there."

"She's slipping in and out of consciousness. Not responding as we speak."

The seconds dragged into minutes.

Reznick cradled her head. "Martha! Martha, you need to wake up!"

Still nothing.

"Goddamn it, Martha, you will wake the fuck up!" He slapped her sharply on the cheek. "Do you hear me?"

Eventually, lights from an NYPD launch pulled up. Four cops on board. Two jumped into the water, waist deep. "Jesus Christ, Jon," one shouted. "You OK?"

Reznick picked up Meyerstein and walked down the beach. He waded in and handed her over to the cops, who got her on board. "Don't worry about me. I'm fine. Get her to hospital right fucking now!"

The launch turned and pulled away, headed back to the mainland.

Sixty-Three

Bill O'Donoghue was stood alone in a windowless conference room as dawn broke, watching Fox News images of police choppers over North Brother Island. Forensics were scouring a wooded area on the deserted island. The anchors spoke of off-the-record briefings, indicating it was a falling-out related to a bitter feud among the Russian mob on the East Coast. The steer had been given by the Feds to the NYPD after details of the operation had begun to leak. And they, in turn, had fed the story to the media.

The Director felt his heart beating hard. Palpitations kicking in. The news from the hospital was not good. Meyerstein had lost a lot of blood. She was critical, still fighting for her life.

His cell phone rang. It was Grady.

"Sir, is it OK to speak?"

"What's going on?"

"I've been reaching out to agencies across the world. Mossad has shared some photos with us, taken a few weeks before Dimitri Merkov was jailed."

"I'm listening."

"He was on vacation in Mexico. Paid a little trip to Tijuana."

"And?"

"Met up with a Serb. I'll send the photos across."

Almost immediately, the surveillance shots appeared on O'Donoghue's screen.

"And this is definitely them?" he said.

"One hundred percent, sir," Grady said. "The money was transferred with the biometric authorization of Merkov junior to the account of a man known as Dragović. A Serb. Assassin for hire. Political assassinations a specialty."

"Tell me, how did this come up?"

"Reznick . . ."

"Reznick? In what way?"

"Reznick asked me a little while ago to get into the account, and track where the money ended up. Face recognition has picked Dragović up in Brooklyn. We believe this is going to go down in New York. Something is afoot."

"When?"

"Imminent."

"Where exactly?"

"Not a clue."

Things were far from over.

Sixty-Four

Just after 8:00 a.m., Reznick was cheered and clapped into the FBI's New York field office by ecstatic colleagues of Assistant Director Martha Meyerstein, who were all relieved to have her found, albeit barely alive.

"Way to go, Jon," a female Fed shouted.

Reznick was mentally exhausted. He forced a smile. He felt uneasy being the center of attention. He much preferred being left to get on with his work. He didn't want thanks. Not even recognition. He just did it because that's what he did. That's what he'd been trained to do.

O'Donoghue took Reznick into his office. He shut the door behind him. "Very good work, Jon."

"It was a close call, let me tell you."

O'Donoghue sighed. "Jon, this isn't over. Not by a long shot."

Reznick blew out his cheeks. "Merkov junior, right?"

"Most certainly." The FBI Director explained what he now knew. The rationale behind Meyerstein's kidnapping, to pressure the Feds to release Dimitri Merkov. The international links to the Russian mob with a known assassin—Andrej Dragović— believed to be on American soil, in New York.

"What else do we know?" Reznick asked.

"They think it's imminent," O'Donoghue said. "We have specialists interviewing Curt White and Brent Schofield, but they claim to be none the wiser . . ."

"It would make sense. Compartmentalize the operation. What was the name of the fuck Schofield was taking orders from?"

"Max Charles."

"Yeah, Max Charles . . . Where is he?"

"No one seems to know. Hasn't been home for days. Family vacationing in Florida. But they don't know where he is."

"Fuck."

"Indeed."

"Charles is ex-CIA, right?" Reznick asked.

"Retired just before the failed Turkish coup."

"Was he linked with that?"

"A few Pentagon neocons, a handful of retired US generals, and a smattering of CIA operatives, yes."

"And we believe this fucker's fingerprints are all over this whole thing?"

O'Donoghue nodded. "We'll find him."

"What is Langley saying to this?"

"Nothing to do with them, apparently."

"Bullshit."

"I'm only repeating what they said. But I'd take what they say concerning this operation with a large pinch of salt."

"Absolutely. This might very well be a shadow operation, run by off-the-books CIA types, non-attributable to Langley. No blowback."

"Perhaps it is . . . That doesn't take away the fact that we have a problem, Jon."

"What about that flash drive of Meyerstein's?"

"We've looked over it. It's very damning. It might merely be guilt by association. But I'll be calling in the investigations division. Stamper withheld that he was CIA. And that is a grave matter."

"Where is he?"

"Upstate penitentiary still. But when he returns, he'll be investigated and his case will be referred to the Inspector General of the

Department of Justice, make no mistake. We need to establish his role in this matter. We'll get to the bottom of this, believe me. But, in the meantime, we have an assassin either in or around New York, preparing to strike." O'Donoghue pressed a key on his laptop, and up on the big screen appeared a picture of the Serb with Dimitri Merkov. "Tijuana. A few weeks before Merkov was arrested."

"Now that's interesting."

"We need to find him. And quick."

Reznick shrugged. "You want me to help?"

"You up for it?"

"Damn right I am. I want to finish this once and for all. Tell me, what do I need to know?"

"This is a whole new ball game, Jon. And you'll play by our rules."

"I can live with that."

"We're hoping that, as we know Dragović is in town, the thousands of surveillance cameras across the city will pick him out."

"I wouldn't count on it."

"Why not?"

"That assumes that assassins look up at surveillance cameras smiling. They know there are cameras everywhere. And they take precautions."

O'Donoghue nodded.

"This fucker—Dragović or whatever his name is—will be well prepared."

"Disguised?"

"Count on it."

Sixty-Five

Vladimir Merkov was sitting on the terrace of his Tribeca duplex, nursing a tumbler of Scotch. Despite the morphine, the cancer was causing him insufferable pain. His life was ebbing away.

Merkov picked up his glass and knocked it back in one. He closed his eyes as he felt himself drifting away. Images of his son as a baby flashed up in his mind.

He opened his eyes and sighed, then turned around and signaled one of his men across. "Boris, do you have the new cell phone?"

Boris handed Merkov the phone.

"Got it yesterday. It's all encrypted, untraceable. But all the numbers you want are on it."

Merkov dialed the number for Max Charles.

"Hey, Merkov, how are you?" Charles said.

"I've felt better."

"I'm hearing that the Feds killed some of your guys and freed Meyerstein."

"You heard correct."

"The operation I'm assuming is still underway, right?"

"Nothing can stop it now. It's been green-lit. We couldn't stop it even if we wanted to."

"I will protect your son, his family, and your associates when you're gone."

"That's all I want to know."

"You have my word."

"The FBI will want blood."

"Let me deal with them." The sound of waves crashing.

"Where are you just now?"

"Offshore."

Merkov smiled. "My favorite place."

"When are we expecting this to be complete?"

"He'll be dead before sunset. That's a promise."

Merkov poured himself another whisky.

Sixty-Six

Dragović smiled as he brushed past the concierge at the Howard Johnson. He had showered, shaved, and changed into the polo shirt and jeans. He was also wearing a Hampers of Hampton baseball cap, which he'd pulled down low. He had injected himself with a beta blocker, which was making him calm.

It was a brisk half-hour walk to the parking garage in the East Village. He saw the vehicle and opened it with the fob. The hamper was in the back, as promised.

He put on his ID lanyard. Then he pulled away slowly and drove uptown. The traffic was slow-moving. Clogged-up. But that was fine.

Dragović's cell phone rang, and the hands-free Bluetooth speaker was activated.

"Yeah," he said.

"Mr. D, how goes it?" The voice of Dimitri Merkov.

"En route."

"Final run-through. The hamper is an icebox containing all the goodies this guy likes."

"I'm listening."

"He's a health-food nut. Reclusive. And that's why he likes all this fancy healthy food delivered to his house."

"What else?"

"Today you will be delivering a variety of dishes. Sticky quinoa porridge with coconut, mango, and lime."

"What the fuck is that?"

"Just listen."

Dragović made a mental note.

"Strawberry and peach bruschetta. And avocado fries with curry-lime dip."

"Fucking hell."

"And not forgetting spring pea and radish salad."

"I get the picture. What's his absolute favorite?"

"Sticky quinoa porridge. And the avocado fries. With . . . a sprinkling of gelsemium."

Dragović grinned. Gelsemium—a rare, toxic Chinese plant—was a weapon of choice for Russian and Chinese assassins. "That will do it."

"Damn right it will."

"What else?"

"We've had our people remotely watching this man in his house for the last six months."

"You guys are thorough."

"Yes, we are. Our intelligence shows that he eats this sort of stuff in one sitting. Then does yoga, watches the stock market for a few hours, and then sleeps."

"He's going for a sleep all right."

"Do good." Dimitri said, ending the call.

Dragović negotiated the traffic until he got to Columbus Circle. Then he turned onto Central Park West, and drove into the parking entrance for number 15. He flashed his ID at security, who waved him through. He pulled up and a valet appeared.

"I'll look after your vehicle, sir."

Dragović took out the hamper first. He was shown into the marble lobby and to the concierge's desk.

"Hey," the concierge said. "Where's Ricky today?"

"He's not feeling too good. I'm covering."

"When's he back?"

"Couple days, I think."

The concierge eyed the hamper. Then he opened it up and looked at the contents.

"Nice and chilled."

Dragović nodded.

The concierge picked up the phone and pressed a few numbers. "Mr. Berenofsky, sorry to bother you, sir, it's Sam in the lobby. Your hamper delivery is here." He nodded and smiled at Dragović. "Very good, sir." He put down the phone. "He's just out of the shower. Take a seat for five minutes, then you can go up."

Dragović grinned. "Thank you so much."

Sixty-Seven

Reznick was pacing O'Donoghue's office. "And the NSA are focused on finding this Serb?"

"Flat-out."

"What's this guy's full name."

"Andrej Dragović."

"Can you pull up his details?"

O'Donoghue pressed a few keys on his laptop and an image appeared on the screen. Reznick stared at the wiry-looking, swarthy man in the picture.

"What do we know about him?"

"Dragović, according to the files, was a Serbian paramilitary, originally part of the Scorpions. The head of the Scorpions was Jovica Stanišić, also head of Serbia's State Security Services, who was, get this, the CIA's main man in Belgrade."

"You're kidding me."

"It was, in essence, a back-channel link to the Serbs, via this guy and the group he headed up."

"So we've got images of this guy with Merkov junior in Tijuana, am I right?"

"Precisely."

Reznick was digesting all the information and piecing it together. "Merkov senior—you think he's now working for the CIA, instead of Moscow, and looking to become a Langley asset, right? And Max Charles has facilitated this whole thing?"

"Precisely. And with Meyerstein as the pawn."

Reznick sighed. "So this guy is in town to do a hit for who? The Merkovs or the CIA?"

"Maybe both. It's a mess. And it's an outrage."

"It's where we are, though. The endgame still eludes us."

O'Donoghue nodded.

Reznick pulled up a seat and sat down. "I know a guy."

"A guy . . . OK?"

"I want to call him. He is a cyber-intrusion expert."

"FBI? NSA?"

"This guy is freelance. He used to work for the NSA. He is a bit unconventional. What he does is borderline illegal. But I would really like to put in a call to him. Do you have any objections?"

"We've got dozens of people who can do this sort of stuff."

"Trust me, this guy is doing prototype surveillance."

"If he's so good, why isn't he still working at the NSA?"

"The pay was lousy, he said."

O'Donoghue took a few moments to consider it. "Make the call."

Reznick pulled out his cell phone. He hadn't called the number since his Delta buddy had been the victim of a Boston Brakes job. Police had called it as drunk driving, ending up with Charles "Tiny" Burns, his wife, and kid dead. But Reznick had learned—with the help of the hacker—that he was in fact murdered by an Iranian hit squad as revenge for taking out nuclear scientists in Tehran.

Reznick paced the office as the number rang and rang. Eventually, after what seemed like forever, a voice answered.

"Yeah?"

"Don't know if you remember me."

A beat. "Reznick, right?"

"First time. Listen, I need your help. Real bad. Time-critical."

"Depends on what this is about . . ."

"I need an assurance that what I say doesn't go outside your little hidey hole in Miami."

"OK, what do you want?"

"We're trying to track down a guy, a foreign national, on American soil. We believe New York."

"Face recognition should've picked him up if you have him on file."

"I would've thought so . . . but it hasn't."

"Why is that?"

"This man is an assassin. And we believe he's about to carry out a terrorist attack. Maybe a hit. We don't know."

"And you've used all face-recognition technology at your disposal?"

Reznick turned and looked at O'Donoghue, who nodded. "Yes, we have."

"Then you got a problem."

"That's why I'm calling. Can you help me or not?"

There was a silence, as if the hacker was considering what he was about to say. "I might."

Reznick felt exasperation. "Look, I haven't got time to play games, my friend."

"I'm working on some software. I hope to patent it later this year, once I've tested it more extensively. This is my intellectual property, so I'm reluctant to give out the details."

"What exactly does this software do?"

"It recognizes people through how they walk. Their gait. And it's phenomenally accurate."

"We've got footage of the guy we're looking for walking in Tijuana."

"Send it to me."

"This is real classified stuff, my friend."

"I'm former NSA, cleared at the highest level. I know all about what you're talking about."

"Where will we send the clip?"

The hacker gave a ProtonMail address.

"Swiss-based, encrypted, right?"

"Exactly, Reznick. Why I use it."

O'Donoghue keyed in the email address and sent the covert footage of Andrej Dragović with Dimitri Merkov in Tijuana.

A few moments later, the hacker spoke. "Which one is which?"

"Dragović, the guy we're interested in, is wearing the pale blue Lacoste polo shirt."

"Cool. What I'm going to do is upload this clip to my secure server, and then run the program I'm developing."

"Then what?"

"Then I'll hack into every surveillance camera in New York, and see if we can get a match."

"How long?"

"Ten, maybe fifteen minutes. But there are no guarantees."

"You speak only to me, on this number."

"I hear you."

The line went dead.

Sixty-Eight

The concierge's phone rang and he picked up. He nodded a few times. "Very good, sir." He hung up and looked across at Dragović. "He'll see you now."

Dragović picked up the hamper. "Thank you."

He walked into the elevator and punched the button for the penthouse level. The doors closed, and he ascended fast. His heart rate was speeding up. He caught his reflection in the metal door.

He was smiling.

This was the part of the job he loved best. The imminent climax of the operation.

Dragović pushed those thoughts to one side as the doors opened. He walked down a corridor to a door at the far end, which was open. A handsome, six-foot-plus man was speaking into a cell phone. He waved Dragović in. Cameras were watching his every move.

"Hope you are well today, sir?" he asked.

Dragović glanced at the living room as he passed. Floor-to-ceiling windows, light flooding through. Central Park, the New York skyline, merging into one.

"Kitchen's at the far end, on the left," the target said. "Just leave it on the table."

Dragović went into the kitchen and placed the hamper carefully on the table. He felt his stomach knot in anticipation.

"So, what's on the menu today?"

Dragović spun around, surprised to see the imposing man standing before him. "A real treat today."

"Like what?"

"Like sticky quinoa porridge with coconut, mango, and lime."

"Sounds great. What else?"

"Strawberry and peach bruschetta. And avocado fries with curry-lime dip. We've also got the most delicious spring pea and radish salad."

The man was grinning, eyes wide. "Love it. I'm absolutely starving." He pulled out a fifty-dollar bill and handed it over. "Thanks a lot."

Dragović gave a respectful bow. "That's lovely, sir."

The man escorted him to the door. "When's Ricky back?"

Dragović had asked for some heavies to kidnap Ricky for a few hours after his first delivery of the day in East Hampton. Then the van had been driven to Manhattan and dropped off in the East Village. "Should be back in a couple days. Pulled a muscle in his back, I think."

"Tell him I was asking after him."

Dragović nodded and walked out. He heard the door being closed and locked behind him.

He got into the elevator and descended, heart fluttering, then walked past the concierge.

"Everything fine?" the guy said.

"Just perfect. Have a good day."

Sixty-Nine

Exactly twenty-two minutes after Reznick called the hacker in Miami, his cell phone rang.

"Jon? Your guy is on the move."

"You managed to find him?"

"Andrej Dragović, according to my software, left the Howard Johnson in Chinatown, one hour and fifty-two minutes ago."

"Where did he go?"

"Parking garage in East Village, picked up a van marked Hampers of Hampton."

Reznick looked at O'Donoghue who was listening, taking notes.

"And you were able to track it from there?"

"Jon, I got him headed direct to Upper West Side, a fancy apartment overlooking Central Park. Owned by a guy called Berenofsky. He lives top floor, penthouse apartment, 15 Central Park West."

Reznick muted the call and turned to O'Donoghue. "Russian oligarch. Saw his picture in *Time*."

"He's more than that."

"How come?"

"I believe he has been providing details of Russian security operatives working in the States. But also their penetration of the financial system."

"So the Russians would want him dead. But why would the CIA?"

"He's due to testify in a month's time, in a closed session of the Senate Intelligence Committee. I'm speculating, but what if he inadvertently gives details of CIA double agents, people like Andrew Sparrow."

"Fuck."

O'Donoghue picked up his phone.

Reznick unmuted the call.

"You still there, Jon?" the hacker asked.

"Sure. Appreciate your help on this."

"That's not all. I've hacked into the surveillance system within 15 Central Park West, where Dragović entered. It appears that someone else was spying on Berenofsky remotely, or at least that's what it looks like."

"Fuck."

"So . . . Dragović emerged from an elevator less than seven minutes ago."

"Fuck. What else do we know?"

"I'm watching Berenofsky as we speak. I'm watching him in real time via the cameras on his cell phone and laptop."

"And what?"

"He's unpacked the hamper that was delivered, and is this minute about to settle down to a pretty large meal with his MacBook beside him, Bloomberg Channel on."

"Listen to me. Pull up the guy's email and phone numbers, right now!"

The sound of tapping on a keyboard. "OK, I'm in."

"Message me with them, do you hear me? He's in danger if he eats that food."

A beat. "Done."

Reznick's cell phone beeped. "Got it."

"Anything else?"

"Stay on the line . . ." Reznick called Berenofsky's cell phone but there was no reply. He called the apartment's landline. Still no one answered. Then he sent a text, telling him to stop what he was doing immediately and call Reznick's number.

Just then, Frankie arrived in the office.

Reznick quickly updated the burly New York Fed, then told him, "You need to get your guys up to the Upper West Side right fucking now." Frankie called his team and got the wheels in motion. "Get paramedics, doctors, and at least six agents up to that apartment, right now!" He ended the call, patted Reznick on the back, and barged out the door. "We're on it."

Reznick still had the hacker on the line. "Now this is really, really important, my friend. Let's leave aside the guy who is about to eat this meal."

"He's just started."

"He's just started eating?"

"Watching some suit talking about oil futures."

Reznick groaned. "Forget him, we've got guys on the way, ready to help him. What I'm interested in for now is Dragović. I need to know where Dragović is."

"You wanna know where the fuck he is?" The sound of typing.

"Right this moment. Where the fuck is he?"

The hacker began to hum. "He's in his little van, headed north."

O'Donoghue gave the thumbs up as his desk phone rang. He picked up and gave the license plate numbers of the Hampers of Hampton van. "NSA has pinpointed this vehicle. He's in uptown Manhattan headed north . . . You on it? Good." He tapped a few keys on his laptop. On the screen, GPS tracking showed the vehicle's route in red on a map of Manhattan.

Reznick spoke into his phone. "We've got this now. That's fantastic."

"Anytime, Jon. Who do I send the bill to?"

"Not so fast. One final favor."

"Name it."

"Vladimir Merkov."

"Who the hell is he?"

"You don't need to know. There's footage we can send to you. I want you to analyze it with this movement software." He turned to O'Donoghue, who forwarded the files to the hacker. "We've just sent it to you."

A beat. "Yeah . . . just landed. OK, so we've got some footage of an old guy . . . in London?"

"That's Merkov, many years back. But it shows him walking, right? And we've also sent footage of his son Dimitri."

"Can't promise anything . . ."

"Do your utmost, that's all I ask."

Reznick ended the call and walked over to look at the map on the laptop screen. "He wants to leave town. Which is the quickest way?"

O'Donoghue stared at the moving red dot. "George Washington Bridge and then across into Jersey."

Reznick said, "We need a chopper."

"Downtown heliport is just five minutes from here. SWAT is already there, standing by."

"I want this son of a bitch."

O'Donoghue took a brief moment, as if reflecting on the situation. "Get on it."

Seventy

Dragović drove across the George Washington Bridge, over the Hudson River, and into New Jersey. He felt good. He would be in Europe this time tomorrow. He envisaged a long vacation by himself. He had a huge villa with an Olympic-sized pool in Marbella. For drinks and dinner, nearby Puerto Banús was perfect.

He thought about Berenofsky smiling at him, grateful for the hamper of healthy, upscale food. And the fifty-dollar tip had been exquisite.

His cell phone rang, snapping him out of his reverie. "Hey . . ."

The voice on the Bluetooth speaker was Merkov junior. "You made the delivery?"

"It's done."

"More like *he's* done. The fuck."

"Whatever."

"Any problems?"

"None at all."

"My people watched the delivery. He won't be seeing the sun come up over Central Park tomorrow, that's for sure."

"Anything else I need to know?"

"Your money . . . The full amount has been transferred."

"Appreciate that, thank you."

"So, where are you headed?"

Dragović sighed. "Going to drop out of circulation for a year or two. But I'm available for any special jobs, any time."

"Your ride out of town is waiting."

"Thank you."

"But there will be a few extra passengers on board."

"As long as I've got a window seat, I'm happy."

The line went dead.

Dragović was on the New Jersey Turnpike. He checked the satnav and got onto I-95. Then he checked his rearview mirror.

He began to smile.

Seventy-One

Reznick adjusted the headset as the chopper, swooping over the Hudson, followed the snaking traffic on the expressway through New Jersey.

The voice of Frankie on the headset: "Jon, do you copy?"

"Go ahead."

"The target is unconscious."

Reznick sighed. "Fuck."

"Barely breathing. Forensics is all over this. We need to wait for toxicology. But the speculation—considering who delivered this food—is that gelsemium might be involved. I seem to remember something similar a few years back."

"You'll be thinking about the Alexander Perepilichny case, near London in 2012."

"Russian tycoon, right? I remember reading about that."

"I heard he had a meeting in Paris, and the Russians poisoned him while he was eating dinner in a restaurant."

"This is the same kind of hit. We need to find this guy. And quick."

Reznick stared down at the cars on the freeway.

"Where exactly are you now?" Frankie asked.

"We're following what we think is Dragović's vehicle, through New Jersey."

"Location?"

"Five miles from Teterboro. What the hell is there?"

"Small airport, Jon."

Reznick was handed some binoculars and caught sight of the vehicle. "I think I can see him." He focused the barrels and saw the Hampers of Hampton van traveling at high speed. "He's not hanging around. That's him all right. And the airport's where he's headed, for sure."

"Problem is," Frankie said, "once he's in, he could be on a flight and in the air in minutes. It's used by Wall Street hedge fund guys with Lear jets on standby."

Reznick knew that if the helicopter landed on the freeway it would potentially end in a fatal crash. He figured they could wait until they reached the airport. Then intercept as Dragović was about to board. But that would be cutting it fine.

"There is another way," Reznick said.

"What?"

"We take him down."

"Jon, that poses multiple risks on a busy freeway. I don't want us getting too gung ho."

"There are risks whatever we do. I can take him down without taking him out."

"How?"

"Do I have the authorization?"

"I need to put you through to O'Donoghue. Hold the line, Jon."

Reznick was put on hold, some Billy Joel piano ballad playing in the background.

"Reznick, it's O'Donoghue. What is it?"

"Sir, I need authorization. Dragović is nearing the airport. I believe a plane will be waiting to take him the hell out of America."

"Can't we land at the airport? Is that an option?"

"Course we could. But I'm telling you, if we lose this guy and let him get away, the critics of the FBI and the American intelligence community are going to have a field day. Again."

"Jon . . . this is high risk."

"Anything we do is high risk. Do I have the authorization?"

A long pause. "Is he aware of your presence?"

"Absolutely. And he's not slowed down. Trust me."

"Very well. Do what you have to—and stop that vehicle."

"I need authorization from the highest level to take him down, if required."

O'Donoghue went quiet for a few seconds. "If required, shoot to kill."

"Copy that, sir." Reznick signaled the SWAT guy beside him. "Gimme your rifle."

"What?"

"Give me the goddamn rifle, son. I'm gonna take this fucker out now."

"Sir, I think it might be better to watch and wait, and get him on the ground."

"Shut the fuck up. I've just been given authorization. Now, are you going to give me the rifle, or am I going to have to take it off you?"

"Man . . . are you kidding me?"

"I'm working on the orders of the Director of the FBI."

The SWAT guy reluctantly handed over the rifle.

Reznick took it and adjusted the sight for windage and angle. He had the car in the crosshairs. But the chopper was shaking, bad. "A bit higher . . ."

The pilot said, "Roger that, sir."

The chopper climbed higher and maneuvered so Reznick had a clear shot of the driver's side.

He stared through the rifle's sight. It was at that moment that Dragović turned and looked up. The Serbian assassin was staring back up at him through the crosshairs.

Reznick had his finger on the trigger.

"Four miles and we're there," the pilot said.

Reznick's headset crackled into life. "Jon . . ." The voice of Frankie. "You're gonna love this. NSA says they've got the location of Dimitri

Merkov from a cell phone conversation with Dragović. He's at the airport . . ."

"You're joking."

"Not at all. He's there."

Reznick held his breath. Suddenly Dragović—one hand on the wheel—raised an Uzi submachine gun and pointed the weapon straight up at the helicopter.

Reznick's instincts kicked in. He squeezed the trigger twice. The shots echoed around the chopper, temporarily deafening him. Dragović's head was blown in half, blood spurting onto the windshield, as the car flipped and crashed into a ball of flames in the middle of the freeway.

Seventy-Two

Vladimir Merkov's limousine pulled up outside the Trex Aviation lobby at Teterboro Airport, and he was greeted by an earpiece-wearing doorman. He was ushered through inside, where it was all beige hues, high glass ceilings, and nice sofas and chairs.

"So, where's my son?"

An associate pointed at the entrance as Dimitri strode in. He wore shades and was flanked by two bodyguards.

Merkov stepped forward and hugged his son. Then he kissed him on the cheek. He held his son's face in his hands as he felt tears spill down his face. "You OK?"

"I'm fine, Dad. I'm gonna miss you."

"This is for the best. You need to get out of the way for a few months."

Dimitri nodded, blinking away the tears. "Dad, I just want to say—"

"You don't have to say anything. We got you out. And we did what had to be done."

Dimitri sighed. "I might never—"

"You need to keep the bloodline going."

"Where am I going?"

"You'll be taken across the border, down to Mexico, and you'll be fine."

"Will I be able to return to the States?"

"Eventually. But not just now. Not for a while. I have people working through this. The plan is in place."

"Are you coming?"

Merkov's heart felt heavy. "Sadly, no. I just wanted you to know that I love you and you can return when this has died down."

"I might never see you again."

"That is correct."

His son stared at him, eyes wet with tears. "I didn't want it to be like this."

"It is what it is."

"The FBI won't forgive or forget."

"Don't worry about them. We have people that can deal with that. Now, your plane is waiting."

Dimitri hugged his father tight, as if never wanting to let him go.

"Enough."

"What about Dragović?"

"Isn't he aboard?"

"I don't know . . ."

Merkov turned and whispered to his associate, who went off to inquire. Then he said to his son, "No time. Get yourself on the plane."

Dimitri shook his father's hand one last time and was ushered through by a doorman to the waiting plane.

Seventy-Three

Reznick's earpiece buzzed as the airport came into view about a mile up ahead, the chopper swooping low. He looked through the crosshairs of the rifle sights.

"Jon, it's your hacker friend on the line," Frankie said. "We're going to patch him through."

"Copy that."

A pause. "Hey, Reznick. Trex Gulfstream waiting on the runway, you see that?"

Reznick saw the Gulfstream, stairs ready for an imminent boarding.

"I've just hacked into their internal radio frequencies, and they're expecting eight people on board. Dimitri Merkov, Dragović, and bodyguards."

Just then, Reznick saw three figures on the tarmac approaching the plane. He spotted the stocky figure of Dimitri Merkov in the middle. He switched his headset to loudspeaker mode. "FBI! Merkov! Freeze!"

A bodyguard spun around holding a semiautomatic, and aimed it at the chopper. Reznick took him out, and then the other armed bodyguards.

Dimitri Merkov stood frozen. Then he turned and made a run for the stairs.

Reznick took aim. He had him in the crosshairs. Fixed in his sights. He tracked the man's run. Then focused on the back of the head. He fired once.

The rear of Merkov's skull was blown off as the thug fell to the ground, blood spilling onto the asphalt.

The chopper hovered as Reznick kept his rifle trained on the approach to the plane.

The pilot said, "Crosswinds coming in, Jon, need to move position."

"Hold!"

"Jon, the chopper is struggling in the crosswinds. We're going to become unstable."

Reznick focused the rifle sight on the bodies. He panned over to the terminal. Suddenly, a skeletal-looking man ran out of the airport terminal and toward the strewn bodies beside the plane. An old man.

Reznick zeroed in. Behind him, a SWAT guy had his rifle trained on the same man. "What do you reckon on the ID of this guy?"

"Fuck."

"That looks like Vladimir Merkov. Can you confirm that?"

The SWAT guy seemed to take an eternity. He checked the photos they had of him. "One hundred percent, Vladimir Merkov. No question."

Reznick watched as Merkov flung himself on his son's dead, bloody body. He lay like that for what seemed like a lifetime. Then he turned and got to his feet and stared up at the chopper. A ghostly smile.

Reznick's finger was on the trigger. He paused as he felt the cold steel on his skin.

"Hands on your head!" he barked through the chopper loudspeaker.

Merkov stood and stared, grinning. Then he reached into his jacket.

Reznick squeezed the trigger twice.

Vladimir Merkov fell backward, hand outstretched as if to touch his dead son, lifeless among the bloody bodies on the New Jersey runway.

Seventy-Four

The hours that followed were like a blur for Reznick as they landed and the New Jersey airport was secured. It was only a matter of minutes before the FBI had designated the area as prohibited airspace. Frankie and his New York Fed guys were quickly on the ground, along with the SWAT team. Forensics a short while after that. There was a total news blackout. The President and his national security advisers were informed.

Reznick was given an extensive debriefing. The murmurings were of summary executions. Reznick shrugged it off.

His role would never be revealed. Not in the recovery of Assistant Director Meyerstein or the tracking and killing of a Serbian hitman. Nor the final justice for the Merkovs.

Reznick didn't want plaudits, anyway. He was taken to a trauma unit to clean up his shoulder wound, bandaged up, and given fresh clothes.

He was finally given the all-clear. He called his daughter and arranged to meet her in a week's time. Then he was driven to a heavily guarded Upper East Side hospital room.

Meyerstein was sitting up in bed, leg suspended by wires and wrapped in plaster. Dark shadows under her eyes.

"Hey . . ."

Reznick took a seat at her bedside. He smiled. "How are you?"

"Doped out of my head, if you must know."

"Lucky you."

Meyerstein smiled. "I was wondering if you were going to show up."

"Had a few things to sort out."

"Like what?"

Reznick explained what had transpired since she'd been retrieved from the island. "So . . . the Merkovs won't be bothering you again."

Meyerstein closed her eyes for a moment.

Reznick looked around. "I spoke to your father, too. He told me about your secret dossier."

Meyerstein nodded. "He wasn't supposed to talk to anyone about it."

"I'm not anyone."

"Indeed, you're not. Was I on the right track?"

"You were more than on the right track. You had it figured out."

"I feel such a fool. How did I not see it? Why didn't I report it to O'Donoghue?"

"How the hell were you supposed to know that Roy Stamper was CIA, and was at Duke with that fuck Curt White?"

"Now that you put it like that . . ."

"What a bastard."

"I'm hearing Roy is already being interviewed. They're going over his house. It's going to get nasty. And if this gets out . . ."

"Do you think he was really doing his job during the investigation into your abduction, or the earlier investigations?"

"We'll find out for sure this time. And I don't think it'll be long. I believe he, and with Curt White, was sabotaging our investigations for CIA purposes. O'Donoghue called me about an hour ago to say Roy had been using a cell phone in his home study for private calls, and there are numerous calls to a number used by Max Charles, former CIA. He also said that Max Charles was more than a million in debt until a year ago. Two disastrous divorces had left him dead broke."

Reznick shook his head. "So he needed money? Wonder if he contacted his old friends at Langley to see if he could do one last job."

"Then again, maybe he was being paid by Merkov, and Charles would be able to deliver Russian assets to the CIA."

"The whole scheme was designed to be impregnable, with Stamper and White blocking any attempt to get near the truth."

"They didn't stop you."

Reznick smiled.

"You're crazy, you do know that, right?"

He looked around her room, with its antiseptic pastel colors. "Love what you've done with the place."

Meyerstein laughed. "Yeah . . . hospital beige. Think it works."

Reznick cleared his throat. "They say you're gonna be fine."

"They say I might walk with a limp."

"Yeah . . . I heard that. But maybe you won't. Maybe the therapists will have you walking just fine."

"It's gonna be painful."

Reznick sighed. "You're alive. I'm glad."

"My ex-husband was in a couple hours ago."

"You have him to thank for getting me involved."

Meyerstein rolled her eyes.

"O'Donoghue said he was expecting you at the congressional hearing in three days' time," Reznick said.

"I thought he might."

"You up for that?"

"Oh yeah, I'll be there."

Reznick nodded. "Nobody need know what transpired."

"Jon . . ." She winced for a moment as she adjusted her position. "I haven't had the chance to thank you."

"Nothing to thank me for."

"I have everything to thank you for. I owe you my life, Jon."

"Hey, just another day at the goddamn office, right?"

Meyerstein smiled. "O'Donoghue is conflicted about you. He says you bring a lot of crossing boundaries and illegality into the equation . . . That said, he told me, just before you arrived, he was sounding me out about creating a role for you with the FBI."

Reznick said nothing. He wondered if a role within the FBI was something that he should consider.

"What do you reckon?"

"Not too keen on roles."

"You could be embedded in our team. A specific job title."

"I'll think about it."

Meyerstein sighed. "In the meantime, what if I wanted to include you in my team in the future?"

"You got my number?"

Meyerstein nodded.

"I'll be there. Somewhere. Waiting."

"Where you off to now?"

"Going back home to Rockland. Maybe have a beer or two. Then I want to sleep. For a long, long time."

Epilogue

Three days later, Reznick was distracted as he sat at the bar of the Rock Harbor Pub with Bill Eastland, nursing a cold beer, trying to watch the congressional hearing on C-SPAN. He listened as FBI Director Bill O'Donoghue and Assistant Director Martha Meyerstein were grilled by the congressmen and women.

Meyerstein looked tired as she outlined the national security priorities she was working on, and the new plans for introducing cutting-edge technology to get the Feds ahead in their fight against organized crime and terrorism.

Eastland sipped his beer. "What you been up to?"

"This and that."

"Figured."

Reznick gulped some of his beer. "Are you setting up a residency at this place?"

Eastland looked around. "It's growing on me."

"What about the beards?"

"Not much of them on show today, so that's a good thing."

Reznick smiled as he watched the coverage.

Eastland looked up at the screen. "FBI, huh?"

"Yeah."

"Don't like the FBI."

Reznick said nothing.

"I said I don't like the FBI."

"I heard you."

Eastland stared at the screen. "What about you?"

"What about me?"

Eastland cocked his head. "You a fan of the FBI?"

Reznick leaned in close and lowered his voice. "I know these two people. And they are good people doing a fucking hard job, let me tell you. So I'd appreciate it if you kept your thoughts to yourself." He picked up his beer and clinked it against Eastland's bottle. "What d'you reckon?"

Eastland looked at the screen. "She's a helluva nice-looking woman."

"That she is. And tough."

Eastland knocked back the rest of his beer. "Great combination."

Reznick gulped down his drink.

"Some things we can't know about."

"Not ever."

"Just the way it is. And for that we should be thankful."

"Damn straight."

Reznick saw Eastland to his house and headed back to his home by the ocean, over a mile away on the outskirts of Rockland. He got in and poured himself a large Scotch.

He picked up his whisky and headed through the French doors and out onto the decking. He sat down on the steps. The waves crashed onto the rocks below. He heard his breathing. The pain in his shoulder was subsiding.

He gulped down the glass of whisky. Then he closed his eyes.

Acknowledgments

I would like to thank my editor, Jane Snelgrove, and everyone at Thomas & Mercer for their enthusiasm, hard work and belief in the Jon Reznick series of books.

Last, but by no means least, my family and friends for their encouragement and support. None more so than my wife, Susan, who offered excellent advice as each draft developed.

About the Author

J. B. Turner is the author of the Jon Reznick series of conspiracy action thrillers (*Hard Road*, *Hard Kill*, *Hard Wired*, and *Hard Way*), as well as the Deborah Jones political thrillers (*Miami Requiem* and *Dark Waters*). He loves music, from Beethoven to the Beatles, and watching good films, from *Manhattan* to *The Deer Hunter*. He has a keen interest in geopolitics. He lives in Scotland with his wife and two children.